"This is a fifteen-round cat-and-dog fight—and O with what zip, verve and wounding laughter the fur doth fly."

—Tom Robbins

"In *Reckless Eyeballing* Reed creates a literary tornado, a book so irreverent and sweeping in its condemnations that it's certain to offend just about everyone."

—Larry McCaffery, *Los Angeles Times*

"Literature is lucky to have Ishmael Reed around. If only for the fun of it."

—David Remnick, *Washington Post*

"Reed is a master of the satirical novel, who takes no single group's side: as usual, he gets everybody. Engaging, disturbing, and really funny."

—*Choice*

"Mr. Reed's fiction bristles with parables, asides, voodoo rituals, razor blades and spikes enough to vex even the most competent plot summarizer."

—Brent Staples, *New York Times Book Review*

"There's something to offend and amuse everyone."

—*Library Journal*

BY ISHMAEL REED

ESSAYS

Writin' Is Fightin'
God Made Alaska for the Indians
Shrovetide in Old New Orleans
Airing Dirty Laundry

NOVELS

Japanese by Spring
The Terrible Threes
Reckless Eyeballing
The Terrible Twos
Flight to Canada
The Last Days of Louisiana Red
Mumbo Jumbo
Yellow Back Radio Broke-Down
The Free-Lance Pallbearers

POETRY

New and Collected Poems
A Secretary to the Spirits
Chattanooga
Conjure
Catechism of D Neoamerican Hoodoo Church

PLAYS

Mother Hubbard, *formerly* Hell Hath No Fury
The Ace Boons
Savage Wilds
Hubba City

ANTHOLOGIES

The Reed Reader
The Before Columbus Foundation Fiction Anthology
The Before Columbus Foundation Poetry Anthology
Calafia
19 Necromancers from Now
Multi-America: Essays on Cultural War and Cultural Peace

RECKLESS EYEBALLING

by Ishmael Reed

Dalkey Archive Press

Library of Congress Cataloging-in-Publication Data:

Reed, Ishmael, 1938-
        Reckless eyeballing / by Ishmael Reed. — 1st Dalkey Archive ed.
            p.   cm.
        ISBN 1-56478-237-9 (alk. paper)
        1. Theater—Production and direction—Fiction. 2. Afro-American dramatists—
Fiction. 3. New York (N.Y.)—Fiction. I. Title.

        PS3568.E365 R4 2000
        813'.54—dc21   00-058956

Partially funded by grants from the Lannan Foundation and the Illinois Arts Council, a
state agency.

Dalkey Archive Press
www.dalkeyarchive.com

Printed on permanent/durable acid-free paper and bound in the United States of
America.

This novel is dedicated to Taj Mahal, David Murray, Allen Toussaint, Steve Swallow, Carla Bley, Carman Moore, Lester Bowie, Kip Hanrahan, Scott Marcus, and all of the others who made the album *Conjure* such a striking success.

What's the American dream?
A million blacks swimming back to Africa
with a Jew under each arm.

—Blanche Knott, *Truly Tasteless Jokes*

1

At first the faces were a blur, but then he was able to identify
the people who owned them. It was a painting he'd seen in a
book about Salem, of the Puritan fathers solemnly con-
demning the witches, but in place of these patriarchs' faces
were those of Tremonisha Smarts and Becky French. He
couldn't hear what they were saying. They were moving their
lips. They were mad. He was sitting in the dock where they
kept the witches. Becky said something to a guard and the
guard started toward him. The guard was about to take him
away to the gallows, he'd gathered from the logic you get in
dreams, but when the guard looked up from underneath the
black Puritan's hat she wore, she wasn't a guard at all but his
mother.

Becky and Tremonisha said cut it, cut it, and then the
dream cut to a scene in the desert. He was cowering behind a
huge cactus plant as a snakeskinned hand was about to cut off
a rattler's head with a large, gleaming blade. He shot up in his
bed. He was sweating. He looked next to him. The cover had
been pulled aside and the woman he'd brought home from the
evening of nonreferential poetry had left. Her subtle perfume
still hung in the air. While he'd been making love to her he
kept thinking of that ad for Jamaica that contained the line:
"Come daydream in a private cove." At one point, they were
fucking so heavy that they began to warble involuntarily like

birds. He'd had about three gin and tonics. This drink always brought out his romance. He got up and put on a robe.

He occupied a large studio in a run-down hotel in the west twenties of Manhattan. A huge poster of Bugs Bunny, carrot in hand, hung over the white fireplace. On a table near the stove and refrigerator lay a box of Kentucky Fried Chicken with only a half-eaten breast and a couple of French fries remaining. The packet of ketchup hadn't been opened. There was a quart bottle of Bombay Gin next to the box. He removed the sheets and blanket from the bed, converted it into a sofa, and added a couple of pillows. On the floor lay a copy of *Life*'s World War II special issue, and a book about negritude poets. On another wall was a Hagler vs. Hearns fight poster. An IBM typewriter, a gift from his mother, lay on a table with more books and magazines. Two magazines with mammoth circulation carried cover photos of Ronald Reagan laying a wreath at Bitburg, a cemetery in Germany where a number of Nazis were buried. A record cover lay on the floor. The Kronos Quartet playing Thelonius Monk's "Crepuscule for Nellie" had played all night. They'd gone to sleep without removing it from the turntable. Underneath that record was one that featured Archie Shepp playing piano, Tadd Dameron's "If You Could See Me Now"; his version was rich and sweet. Most of the records in his collection were from the Caribbean, but he loved jazz, be-bop, and blues as well. They'd gone to a Clifford Jordan performance after the reading; he invited her up to his hotel room for "conversation." He told her that she didn't talk like an American. He remembered that he had told her she looked like an Arawak Indian. That's why the opened map lay on the floor next to the subway tokens. He had brought out this map of the Caribbean to show her were the Arawaks were located. Sometimes when you're inspired you'll say anything, Ian thought. The dishes in the sink were giving off a sour odor. He fixed himself a cup of coffee and sat on the sofa after turning on the Sony 25-inch, also a gift from his mother.

His mother had second sight. Once when they were having an argument she had blurted out, Maybe I don't have such a grand education as you but there are some things that I know that your professors and all your high-class education don't know. She could know your business before you knew it. One of the reasons he came to New York from the South was to become a playwright. The other was to get away from his mother. Being the son of a mother who had what the people in Arkansas called "the Indian gift" was not easy. When he was a kid he couldn't get away with a thing. He had the vague feeling that even here she was noticing him, and knew what he was up to. The phone rang. Speaking of the devil.

"Are you all right, Ian? I had a bad dream about you. You aren't getting those women mad at you again, are you?" How did she know that? Ian wondered. "I'm one step ahead of you, Ma," he said. "I've written a play that's guaranteed to please them. The women get all of the good parts and the best speeches. I've taken all the criticism they made of *Suzanna* to heart. You'd be proud of me. I'm—I'm going for it."

"You what?"

"I'm trying to reform, Ma."

"Don't be using that low-class vulgar Yankee talk on me, you hear? When you coming home? End this artistic foolishness. It's been six years since you left the South. I worry about you up there in New York."

"I'm here for the limit, Ma. I'm going to make it as a playwright. I can't quit now. They're doing my play at the Lord Mountbatten. Anyway, I have to go to a meeting with my director. I'll call you later."

"Did you get the check?"

"Yeah, thanks, Ma. And, look, this time I think I've got a hit. You won't have to send me any more cash."

"That's what you said the last time. Before *Suzanna*. Don't get me started on that."

"Goodbye, Ma." He put the receiver down. He put on some jeans and a sweater.

There were real problems growing up with a clairvoyant mother. A woman who could look around corners and underneath the ground. He used to have nightmares of eyes with wings swooping down on him. Then the room would be full of women wearing white dresses and white head coverings. And then he would be at peace again as they knelt, rocked, and keened about his bed in a circle. He cleaned up the place, leaving the chore of putting away the gin until last. He took a swig of the gin, twisted the cap on, and put it on a shelf above the sink. Actually he preferred rum. He walked out to get the newspaper. What it carried on the front page woke him: TREMONISHA SMARTS, WELL-KNOWN BLACK PLAYWRIGHT, ACCOSTED BY PSYCHO. He read the story. It said that a man dressed in a gray leather coat, matching beret, and dark glasses had entered Tremonisha Smarts' apartment two nights before, tied her up, and shaved all of her hair off. His twisted explanation: this is what the French Resistance did to those women who collaborated with the Nazis. The man had said that because of her "blood libel" of black men, she was doing the same thing. Collaborating with the enemies of black men. Ian blinked and read the story again.

2

It was a blue and windy New York day. Jim's scarf almost reached his hips. He had his hands in his pockets as he walked and half ran toward the theater. His black curls seemed to bounce on his head. As he bounded up the stairs, he didn't acknowledge the greeting of two actors who were descending. Mr. Ickey, Becky's assistant, tried to block his way but was unsuccessful. When Jim burst into Becky's office, she became as angry as he was, but managed to put on a professional smile. The German shepherd she kept tied to the leg of her desk stood up and began some ugly barking. She commanded him to sit down. Becky had two guests, an elderly woman with gray-silver hair tied up into a bun and wearing a black velvet dress and black shoes, and the woman's chauffeur, a huge, oafish-looking man with gray hair. He looked as though he weighed about 250 pounds.

"Oh, Jim, I'd like you to meet—"

"I didn't come here to meet anybody. I came to talk to you."

"What about?" The smile vanished. She was wearing a black dress with a long, white, pointed collar.

"Ickey called me this morning and said that you were going to consider moving Ball's play to the Queen Mother," Jim said.

"I have a new play. A play that I'm very excited about," Becky said. The old lady smiled.

"Yes. I read the newspaper. Eva Braun. What are you celebrating that Nazi whore for?" The old woman's cane fell, making a klooking sound on the hardwood floor. She was shaking. The chauffeur scrambled toward the cane and picked it up. The corners of Becky's mouth were twitching. Her skin became red.

"She may be a Nazi whore to sexists like you, but to many of us, she epitomizes women's universal suffering." She was trembling.

"What? You must be out of your mind. She was married to Adolf Hitler?"

"She was coerced. Just as all women are coerced by men into doing things against their will."

"Must be written by one of your neurotic feminist friends. You let them use the Mountbatten as some kind of playpen where they can mudsling their invective at men, but you would deny the Mountbatten to Ian Ball." Jim and Becky were now leaning on the desk and shouting at each other.

"We disagree about that. His play is . . . well, it reads like a first draft."

"Who are you to decide the merits of his play? You're just a glorified reader around here. You stupid *shiksa*. It's my directing that draws the numbers, and the numbers get the grants." The dog was on its feet again. Jim and Ian had laughed as they fantasized about the relationship between Becky and her German shepherd. They had said foul, unprintable things.

The old lady whispered something to her chauffeur. He got up and left the room, giving Jim a nasty stare as he exited. Becky began to sob. Jim shifted his eyes in annoyance, first to the portrait of William Shakespeare on the wall, then to the slim vase holding the tulips on Becky's desk.

"I expect to do *Reckless Eyeballing* in the Mountbatten, and if you stand in my way I'll break your neck." Jim stormed from the room.

He almost collided with the chauffeur, who was returning with two Diet Coke cans. He gave one to the old woman. Becky recovered her composure as she spoke to her guests.

"I don't have to tell you how sorry I am about this intrusion, but these New York Jews are just . . . just brazen. They have the manners of the lowly peddlers they are. I don't know what we're going to do with them. But don't worry, Ms. Smith, with your contribution we won't have to worry about donations from those people anymore. You can count on the Mountbatten. He doesn't know it, but I've already begun casting." The old woman's stiff hands removed the checkbook from her purse; she began to write her signature. Becky smiled and studied the piece of paper that would pay the Mountbatten's expenses for two years. The woman ripped the check from the checkbook and handed it to Becky.

"I still think that you should acknowledge the authorship of the play. The press has been calling. A few interviews might boost ticket sales." The old woman shook her head.

"As you wish," Becky said. The dog and the chauffeur were staring at each other. Finally the dog looked askance and began to whine and wag its tail. The chauffeur laughed and continued to drink from the can.

Detective Lawrence O'Reedy, "Loathesome Larry," as he had been nicknamed by generations of admiring rookies (he'd always confront a criminal with his personal snub-nosed .38, Nancy, with the threat, "Give me something to write home to Mother about"), lumbered into the lobby of a fashionable East Side condominium (both down payment and maintenance costs pretty steep) located near the United Nations Plaza, around the corner from Danny Johnson's obelisk for Ralph Bunche. The black doorman gave him some lip, but O'Reedy knocked him to the floor with one punch to the stomach. The doorman, Randy Shank, fell to his knees and held his stomach in agony. O'Reedy was all out of breath when he reached the elevator, and so leaned against the wall, waiting for the elevator to reach the first floor. He was thinking about Florida. In six months he'd retire to Vero Beach and be seated in a deck chair, dressed in golf shorts and Hawaiian shirt, staring out over the reef. Just a few more cases and he'd be out of New York, which had become a toilet for all the human offal of the world. Wasn't like the old days when men were men and you could separate the men from the boys. Nowadays, you just about had to read a criminal a bedtime story before you arrested him. He thought of all the P.R.s and nig—or blacks, as they were calling them these days—he'd arrested. He'd spread-eagled and frisked. The brains blown out. The days when men were men. Been a long time since he'd been one himself. He was even thinking about consulting a Chinese herbalist. Nothing had solved the problem. His wife, Betsy, the Lord bless her. She was patient. She had her women's club and charities.

His esophagus was always burning, and he ate a lot of hard candy because someone had told him that hard candy was effective in treating flatulence. Recently he was having bad dreams in which he'd seen the faces of the dead he'd dispatched to the land of ghosts, blown-up before him. And then, this morning, was it a man, with a part of his skull missing and blood on his shirt, in his house, sitting in his chair, reading his newspaper? It looked up from the newspaper and grinned at O'Reedy, a mass of putrefying flesh hanging from its skull. He screamed and ran back into the bedroom to grab Nancy. Betsy said that she was sure that he was just having a nightmare, but when he went back to get the newspaper, the man had gone, yet the newspaper was scattered about the floor and not outside, on the doormat, folded neatly. Must have been the spaghetti and meatballs he ate the night before. The way he looked at it, those men deserved to die. I mean, they were running away, weren't they, so they must have been guilty. Well, maybe that black jogger was innocent, but it was dark the morning he shot him. He couldn't see so well, and besides there had been a number of rapes in that park. Everybody knew that all black men did was rape white women, so too bad for the jogger, but, well, the way O'Reedy looked at it, this was war, and in war a lot of innocent people get killed. But then, the other day he had opened the shower curtain and those three P.R.s he'd shot one night after a rooftop chase

were standing there in the shower, nude, and singing some
song in Spanish, and the bullet holes were still visible on their
chests, and he didn't understand the Spanish. What really
haunted him was the jogger's name: O'Reedy, same as his.

Tremonisha Smarts opened the door upon the detective
who'd come to investigate. She'd called after the intruder left.
She'd freed herself from the ropes with which he'd tied her
into a chair. The detective was breathing heavily. He was a
medium-sized man, and was wearing a brown hat with a band
of darker brown. He wore a starched white shirt and plain,
dull tie. His black shoes had been shined. His lower lip pro-
truded and some of the membrane was exposed. His jaws were
slack, and he had a nose that was crooked in the center as
though it had been repaired. He identified himself as Detective Lawrence O'Reedy of the New York Police Department.
He tipped his hat and smiled at the woman, who was dressed
in a manner that revealed much "eye candy," as people in
advertising said. Her head was covered with some white cloth
made of what appeared to be a rich fabric. She wore some
earrings and bracelets. Tremonisha Smarts. His wife had insisted that he see her play, *Wrong-Headed Man*. She thought
that he'd fall asleep, but it turned out that he rather enjoyed it.
Especially the scene where the big black ape throws his missionary wife down the stairs. Tremonisha was sobbing. She
said something like, "I'm glad you came," and said it in such a
manner that got him excited. She guided him into the living
room of the large, high-ceilinged apartment and led him to a
seat. O'Reedy slowly lowered his huge bottom into a chair and
removed his notebook and pen. "Would you like a drink?" she
asked.

"Scotch," he said. She disappeared into the kitchen. There
were some paintings on the wall, and some posters from her
play *Wrong-Headed Man* that depicted the controversial scene
where Mose, the lead character, stands at the top of the stairs,
arms folded and a cigarette dangling from his lips, while at the

bottom his missionary wife, whom he has pushed down the stairs, lies sprawled and sobbing, her dress up around her waist. Throughout *Wrong-Headed Man*, Mose goes on a spree of woman-bashing rape and incest. A pain shot through O'Reedy's kidneys. He grimaced. "Is anything wrong?" Tremonisha asked, his drink in her hand. O'Reedy didn't acknowledge the remark. "Could you give me a description of the man?" he asked.

Sometimes O'Reedy went for days without evacuating his wastes and when stools did show up, they were dark and pasty. His wrists were always in pain. Yet it seemed like only yesterday that he calmly drove through the car dealer's showcase window to capture some niggers who were inside, holding a white woman as hostage. That was the day he became a legend. He had pulled his pet heat Nancy on the niggers, and before pasting their insides to the wall he said: "Give me something to write home to Mother about," the line that became immortal, even quoted by politicians. Hey, he was even mentioned on one of the syndicated shows. "In the news recently, there was an incident involving three hoodlums and a New York City detective. What did the detective say before shooting all three?" The lady answered the question correctly and won fifteen thousand dollars. When O'Reedy had lifted the hysterical woman hostage to her feet and led her outside, the noonday crowd had applauded. That was the year the public, making its wishes known through the polls, had pleaded with him to run for mayor.

"He was a large man. He wore a raincoat, white scarf, and beret. He wore dark glasses. He had the cheekbones of a well-fed cat, and, and . . ." Tremonisha began to cry. O'Reedy looked up from his notepad. She was wearing silk pajama–type pants, white blouse, and a white turban to cover the damage that her assailant had wrought. She had big eyes and long, dark eyelashes.

"He said all sorts of political things. Said that I was giving the black man a bad name." (O'Reedy offered her a handkerchief. She declined and took some fancy department store tissue that rested in a pink box on the table next to the chair. She blew her nose.) O'Reedy felt like taking her into his arms, comforting her, and saying things like, "Now, now."

"Probably some psycho with wounded masculine pride," O'Reedy said, writing down his observations in his notebook. A political nut. "Outside of the hair . . . did he harm you in any other way?"

"No, as a matter of fact he left me this." She showed the detective a chrysanthemum. The detective took it from her and put a handkerchief about it.

"I'll take it down to the lab. He must have some kind of obsession with hair. Why would he cut your hair?"

"He said that the hair was cut because that's what the French did to the women who collaborated with the Nazis during the war."

"Looks like we have a real lunatic here." He leaned over and clasped her moist hand. He felt some nerves stirring in his left hand. The hand that had gone numb many years before.

"It's a shame that he did this to you." He looked up at the turban; he felt like patting her head, but he restrained himself. She smiled and blushed. "Don't worry, Ms. Smarts. I'll get the bastard if it's the last thing that I do." The phone rang. She walked over to pick it up. The detective glanced at her serendipitous buttocks moving beneath her silk pants. His eyes moved from left to right.

"I can't talk to you now. Tomorrow, Towers. It'll have to be a late flight. You'll arrange it? Why do you keep asking that question? It's fiction, I told you—you keep asking me did it really happen? No, I never had incest with my father. I'm becoming annoyed, Towers. Yes, I'll have dinner with you tomorrow." She hung up and nervously plucked a cigarette from a box on the table. O'Reedy lit the cigarette. "They're doing a film of *Wrong-Headed Man*," she said finally, blowing out smoke.

Ian Ball's friends, the black male writers whom he referred to as the fellas, had observed that since the film version of *Wrong-Headed Man* was being produced, directed, and written by white males, that they, the fellas, could look forward to a good media head-whipping just about the time the film came out. They imagined that the white feminist critics were already lining up to review it, queuing up like those people who wait all night for the opportunity to buy a ticket to a Prince concert, even feuding about which one was going to be the first to drub old Mose. Skin Mose—the American black man—alive.

"My wife and I saw it," O'Reedy said. "That scene—you know the one where the huge black brute throws this mulatress down the stairs, but not before—you know where she is lying there begging for mercy when he—I started to run up on the stage, it was so realistic. All I could think to do was rescue that woman—ever since I saw that, I was wondering, Ms. Smarts, did that really happen? I mean, did some black brute take you—I mean, how was it?"

"Mr. O'Reedy, I really have to be packing. I'm flying to Hollywood tomorrow. I still have to do revisions on the script. Will you be needing me?"

"I think I have enough information. Please call me when you return. We might have some additional clues. We'll do everything we can to stop this creep."

"Thank you, Detective O'Reedy." He rose and wobbled to the door, placing the notebook into the pocket of his gray gabardine overcoat. He tipped his brown hat and smiled.

4

"Good grief, look at the tits on that one," Jim said.

"Jesus. Would you look at that. I'd like to take that one for a horseback ride all night long. Yeeeeooowww." Ball and Jim had just finished their work on the play and were looking at the photos of some of the women who had been cast.

"So as I was saying, the guy from the outer office, you know, Ickey, he comes rushing in — was he livid. He looked like he wanted to fight, but she told him it was all right. They had this big, beefy-looking guy with a crew cut there. Bluest eyes I ever saw. He's the old broad's chauffeur and bodyguard. His name is Otto. I thought he was going to jump into it, but he didn't say anything. Anyway, I'm screaming at this broad and she's just standing there."

"Man. I would have loved to see the expression on Ickey's face. He is one bigoted bastard. He called my stuff crude. I'd like to crude him." Ian took another hit of the joint and passed it to Minsk. Ian did an imitation of Ickey that wasn't too complimentary. They both laughed. Minsk leaned back and almost fell out of the kitchen chair.

"Imagine that twat. Thought she could get away with it. Do this Eva Braun play at the Mountbatten and give you the Queen Mother."

"How did you hear that she was going to try it?"

"I was sitting in a café around the corner from the theater and I heard these two broads talking about it. They were ex-

cited about the Eva Braun thing. They said that you were . . .
are you ready for this? A notorious sexist."

"I can see why they would say that about my first play,
Suzanna, but they'll have to change their minds after they see
Reckless Eyeballing. They're going to have to like Cora Mae's
monologue."

"Man, are the sisters going to get you for that," Minsk said.
Ball thought for a moment.

"I know. But I figure if I can win these *white* broads to my
side, the sisters will follow. The few who think the way they do
are dependent upon them. You know how Becky first promoted Johnnie Kranshaw, and then when Johnnie Kranshaw
disappeared after a falling out with Becky and her friends, they
brought in Tremonisha, and last word I got was that they're
tired of the black American women because they feel they
can't be trusted and are 'surly,' and so they're going to start
importing some black women from the Caribbean who'll be
more agreeable and do their bidding for them. Deputize them
to go out and smear black men. At least that's what Brashford
said."

"Yeah, well, they're hard on us white males, too." Ball
stared at Minsk for a moment.

"Brashford says that you're not a white male, you're Jewish,
that white men and Jewish men have been fighting for cen-
turies and for you to call yourself a white man is strange. He
says that just because you know about Wallace Stevens and
Chekhov doesn't mean that these people are going to accept you as white, no way."

They'd been through this before. Minsk used to argue about
universality and the minimal importance of ethnicity, but that
would only encourage Ball to quote more of Brashford's rant-
ing and raving.

"He reminds me of my father. He's paranoid too."

"Yeah. Brashford does go off the deep end from time to
time. How's your father doing?"

"The President's visit to Bitburg really upset him. First it was the Nativity Decision, you know where the Supreme Court ruled that the display of Christian symbols is a legitimate part of the American Christmas. He said that every Jew was going to find his exit and he'd find his in death. He thinks that the Christians are going to make Jews convert or leave the United States."

"Well, maybe he has a point."

Minsk got up and went to the small refrigerator in his bachelor's kitchen and got a bottle of beer. He was about five-foot-nine-inches and weighed 150 pounds. He went about his house in a jumpsuit and ate 100 percent bran every morning. There were fern plants in his bathroom and health food store soaps.

"I don't think so," he said to Ball when he returned to the living room. "He was in some pogrom. This whole town was murdered by the Cossacks."

"Pogrom? What are you talking about?"

"The Europeans were massacring Jews before they went into Africa after the blacks. Ancient Christians hated the Jews. They were suspicious of them because they wouldn't mingle with them or worship their gods. At least that's one theory. In Russia, where my folks came from, discrimination against the Jews was especially virulent, though sometimes they were tolerated; depended upon which czar was in power."

"Well, all of the Jews over here seem to be eating good. Nobody's herding them into ghettos. What was wrong with your old man?"

"It happens to old people. They get disoriented. You know. My uncle, his younger brother, says that Pop always acted old. He'd go down to the deli or the automat where some of these old-timers would read and discuss the newspapers and talk about the old days in Russia. He'd spend hours there. Or he'd have his head buried in some books. He wrote poetry in Yiddish. He clung to the old ways while everybody else became assimilated, including my uncle, who used to be a gangster. You can't get any more assimilated than that."

"I didn't even know you had an uncle," Ball replied.

"Guy was in the mobs, up until before World War Two. Went to St. Louis and opened up a chain of carpet stores."

"A gangster. In your family?"

"Surprised me too. I thought all of the gangsters were Irish or Italian. But there was some guy named Dutchman. He was a Jew. He ripped off Harlem for millions of dollars. Rigged the numbers so that he was always guaranteed a hefty take."

"Jewish gangsters. I thought all the Jews were slumlords." Ball grinned.

"Sure. Einstein, Trotsky, Chagall—slumlords. Fuck you, Ball."

"Hey, look, man. You're the one who says he doesn't affiliate," Ball said. "So what are you so sore about? Gimme a break."

"I just hate misinformation, Ian. The Jews own the media, the Jews own the garment district, the Jews own this, the Jews own that. They just libel Jews with that shit so's to take their minds off of those who really own it. That's the same shit they used against you blacks. Like the black welfare queen with the fur coats and two homes and diamonds."

"Okay. Okay. Jim, look, man, I take it back."

They were silent for a minute, both of their heads buried in the script.

"I'm surprised that we got Cora's monologue past Becky. She suggested that Cora Mae's line here on page forty-one read something about her victimization by both the Reckless Eyeballer, Ham Hill, and by her husband. She said that because he leered at Cora the black was just as guilty as the white men who murdered him," Jim said.

They broke up and the joint they smoked made them laugh even harder.

"She wanted to—I can't believe it. What a screwy bitch.

The man who reckless eyeballed the woman, so she claims, is just as guilty as the men who murdered him. That has got to be the most outrageous crap. Where do broads like that get off?" Ball said. They both laughed until they cried.

"Hear about Tremonisha?" Minsk asked.

"Yeah, it's all in the newspapers and on TV. Man, the fellas are very bitter. They're not going to stand for it, according to Brashford. I mean, they just about fought that Vietnam War single-handedly, them and some poor whites, while these middle-class white guys were backing them up in some kind of moving country club at Cam Ranh Bay. These broads should know that the only thing standing between them and these gooks and things that want to strangle them in their sleep is the fellas. At least that's the way Brashford sees it."

"She said that rapists ought to be castrated," Minsk said, his eyes probing Ball's for a response.

"Half the white boys in the country would be walking around with no dicks if it came to that. They the champs at date rapes and trains. Look at these white boys knocking over these nursery schools left and right—fucking little children in the butt—how sick can you get, fucking pineapples and dead people. You should hear Brashford talk about it."

"He didn't see it that way. The Flower Phantom took it personally," Jim answered. Ball tried to restrain his grudging admiration for the man who had accosted Tremonisha, the man the media was calling the Flower Phantom for his habit of leaving a chrysanthemum with his victim.

"Sounds like a real screwball. My mom always taught me to respect women," Ball said.

"Yeah, I admire that bond you have with your mother. I was never that close to mine. She was always speaking in Yiddish. Feeding the poor. I was afraid to bring friends home. Afraid she would embarrass me. You say your mother's clairvoyant?"

"Yeah, a couple of scientists checked her out. Physicists."

"What?"

"I kid you not, man. These guys came out from some school and did tests on her. She's got it. When I was a kid, I couldn't get away with a damned thing. I always wondered how did she know that. Man, did I get a lot of spankings. She'd spank me before I'd even do anything. She'd get all dressed up in black and just appear with a switch in a room where I was into some mischief. Like I'd look up and there she'd be. Gave me the creeps. Anyway, these two dudes say that they are beginning to understand the behavior of particles that communicate with each other faster than the speed of sound, and if you're close to someone like a family or a wife or something, the particles are familiar and communicate even faster. It's possible that you could experience an event before it even happens. They call it precognition. They say that's the way telepathy works. Some people's particles communicate quicker than others, because there is less debris surrounding their auras, they have clean auras, or something like that.

"Anyway, I used to didn't listen to her, me having gone to college and all, but now when she says something, I listen. She said that in the 1970s there'd be a deep recession, and she was right. See, the Africans are into guardian spirits. These spirits of the deceased seem to be central to African psychology, that the world is peopled by spirits of the dead, millions of them, and they intrude into man's experience. Give him advice, on how to hit the numbers. Some people are just born conductors. My mother is one."

"Yeah," Minsk chuckled. "We call them dybbuks."

"Dybbuks, huh. Well, maybe that's what happened to your old man. Your old man was listening to some dybbuk. Maybe he's right. Maybe these white people are going to tighten the screws on the Jews. Brashford says he keeps his passport renewed, because the way the country is moving, he wouldn't be surprised if they started up slavery again. He said that they're pushing the clock back to the pre–Civil War period. Right now we're in the 1880s."

"Brashford. You listen to him a lot."

"You don't like him, do you?"

"His talent isn't all that large. His only play is warmed-over O'Neill. *The Iceman Cometh.* All of that stuff about illusion and reality. And the one scene taking place in the bar. The reason they went for it in the fifties was because the last monologue was delivered by a black guy got up in drag. Everybody knows that. That's why he's such a darling of the East Coast establishment."

"Well, why can't he steal from O'Neill? The white boys steal our shit. Brashford says that you got these sixty-year-old punk rockers saying that they invented jazz poetry and blues. The ones in their late thirties, the yuppies with their Brooks Brothers suits and things, are saying that they invented rock and roll, and some of the white dudes in their seventies claim ragtime." Minsk looked at the clock. He had to get to the airport. When Ball said something to annoy him, Minsk would either change the subject, pretend that he didn't hear, or come up with something else to do.

O'Reedy was seated at his desk. Tremonisha Smarts was lying on a sofa. She was dressed in a magenta-colored gauzy gown. Her thighs and tits—well, you didn't have to strain all that much to see them. She was beckoning him. Reaching out to him. Enticing him to join her on the sofa. She even patted a place next to her, a seat she intended for him to have. O'Reedy was dressed in a tux, which fit just right, and shiny black shoes. He began to float toward her. Soon they were engaged in a mean tango, their bodies riveted. Someone cleared his throat, awakening O'Reedy from his reverie.

"Yes, what is it, Brown?" An Afro man, with keen features, a thick mustache, dressed in pants with well-defined creases and a splendid white shirt and striped tie, a shoulder holster fastened to his chest. He was holding some papers in his hand.

"The newspapers are calling him the Flower Phantom."

"What?"

"The Flower Phantom."

O'Reedy rustled the papers with annoyance. He tilted his head and slitted his eyes. "You're not becoming sympathetic to this degenerate pile of shit, are you, Lieutenant?"

The young man snapped to attention. He straightened up. "No, sir."

"Then what's the problem with you? Is it because you're both black! Speak up, Brown!"

"No, not at all, sir."

"Just because you're both black, you must remember that he's a criminal and you're on the side of the law. He's on the outside, you're on the inside. Never forget that."

Brown was embarrassed. "Sir, it's just that, well, a lot of the fellows don't like Tremonisha Smarts. She wrote that play *Wrong-Headed Man*. A lot of the fellows are saying that her portrayal of the brothers, well, you know, they're saying that it's not too cool. She makes out like we're all wife beaters and child molesters. I mean, I don't beat my wife. And that scene where Mose throws the woman down the stairs."

"Did you see the play, Lieutenant?"

"No, sir, but—"

"Go see the play, especially that scene—well, you know, well, there's a scene—look, we're here to protect the public, not to be theater critics. How old are you, anyway?"

"I'm thirty-two, sir," the lieutenant said. O'Reedy sighed. Just a kid, he thought.

"Lieutenant, I have a lot of paperwork, if you will excuse me."

"Yes, of course, sir." The young lieutenant left the office, O'Reedy's eyes following him. O'Reedy was looking forward to his retirement. It couldn't come soon enough. The force certainly had changed. Along about the mid-seventies some meddlesome wimp of a judge had decreed that every time a white policeman achieved a promotion, they had to promote a black. Sure, police brutality complaints were on the decline, but that wasn't the point. In the old days you roughed them up so that they'd realize that white men were in charge. You didn't take any crap in those days. If they'd had this civilian review jazz in the old days, he and the boys would have seen to it that none of the complainants survived to file a complaint. He thought again about the time, decades before, when he had dropped those three bank robbers while finishing up his sandwich. If memory served him correctly, it was a bacon, lettuce, and tomato sandwich on whole wheat bread. He remembered all of the events of that day and played them over and over again in his mind. The screams, the blood and human tissue splattered all over the place. He kept blasting, and the black sons of bitches were flying in all directions, and the crowds were screaming. When he finished his sandwich, he went inside the restaurant and ordered another one. Cool as he could be. Squint-eyed and disdainful.

The whole Western World was becoming sissy. What did that sell-out Jew, Henry Kissinger, say? Something about the Western World going to the dogs, and how his job was to make it easier for the West to accept this. He'd read this in the Sunday paper. What kind of thinking was that? Jew thinking, that's what it was. Used to have somebody around the department who agreed with him, but now all the fellows had left, gone to Vero Beach, Florida. Soon he'd join them.

Sure, they wasted a lot of the "underclass," but in the old days the mayor and the head of the Police Benevolent Association would take your side. And if you, well, had to remove some poor slob from his misery, there was always the friendly M.E. who'd fix it up. Nowadays, the head of the Police Benevolent Association was a woman. Sanchez . . . Chavez . . . something like that. Lawrence O'Reedy dropped to one knee, pulled his gun, and mockingly pointed it at an imaginary fleeing suspect. "Freeze, you son of a bitch. Give me something to write home to Mother about." He chuckled to himself. He got up and tugged on his pants at the waist. Brown was standing in the doorway, a puzzled expression. "You all right sir?" he asked.

6

Ball entered the plush building in which Jake Brashford's intown studio was located. He had a home on Long Island where it was claimed that he stashed away his wife and child. None of the fellas had seen them. The doorman looked him up and down before phoning up to Jake and having Jake verify his appointment. The doorman kept reading his newspaper as he nodded in the direction of the elevator. *The New York Pillar* said: "Flower Phantom Strikes Again." Ian had read the paper that morning. The Flower Phantom had tied up the editor of a feminist magazine and shaved her head.

When he got off the elevator a well-tailored white woman

was heading in the direction of the elevator. When she saw Ball she turned around and half trotted in the opposite direction. Ball was a large man with broad shoulders. He had large hands and ripe facial features. To some he might have resembled a large ape.

Brashford opened the door. He was slight with a thin mustache. His face was a reddish-brown color, and he had freckles: from his Irish ancestors, he claimed. He was always carrying on about the Cherokee and Irish in his background, and to skeptics would point out the famous black people with names like McCovy, MacElroy, Kennedy, McClure, McRae, and Shaw. He was frowning as usual, his hands in the pockets of his smoking jacket. The apartment was large and contained expensive furniture but very little of it. There were paintings on the wall that had been given or lent to him by friends from his generation. There were a number of books by Russian authors on his shelves. Dostoyevsky. Turgenev, whom Dostoyevsky accused of lacking ethnicity, and the old man Gogol, who ridiculed the modernist dogma that characters be "well rounded." There was so much O'Neill memorabilia that the apartment seemed to be a shrine to the dark Irishman. In one room hung a huge portrait of Paul Robeson in Napoleonic military jacket and tights. An album cover on the top of the sleek blond (thirty thousand dollar) stereo system showed Louis Armstrong squint-eyed and grinning in an ambassador's formal clothes. There were a number of books by American transcendentalists lining the bookshelves, plus oversized technical books on lighting, equipment, and stage design.

Brashford snickered. "Man. Why don't you get you some vines. You look like one of those punk people with them jeans and that leather jacket. I'm glad you stopped wearing that cowboy hat. Boy, they're right. You can take the nigger out of the country, but you can't take the country out of the nigger." Brashford wouldn't end a conversation with anybody without mentioning this adage at least twice. And he was so out of touch that he thought people still said "vines." Brashford always recommended that Ian consult his personal tailor. "I'll pay for it," he had promised.

"I started not to let you up here. I've been working on my second play," Brashford said.

That's a laugh, Ian thought. He'd been telling people for years that he was at work on a second play, but even his strongest supporters realized that he would never finish the play, because he was afraid that the patrons who had lavished him with gifts, prizes, chairs, would abandon him if it weren't as big a hit as his first play, *The Man Who Was an Enigma*. In other words, he was afraid of failure, so the fellas said.

After directing Ball to a seat, Brashford plopped down in the lap of his favorite sofa. Ball came right to the point.

"You've had the manuscript for about a month now, Jake. I wanted to get your reaction."

"You want to get a reaction to your new play, huh? You and about thirty thousand others. See those corners? People think all I have time for is to read their manuscripts and scripts. I had to hire an extra secretary just to stand in line at the post office and at the copy places. See those corners?" He pointed to a corner of the room with his eyes.

"You and these other people calling me from all over the country asking me to read their manuscripts. You guys think that I'm some fucking agent. Get an agent.

"Anyway, what's all of this Ham shit? Ham Hill." Bradford chuckled, then returned to his usual poker face. "You country boys come up here and try to wax all intellectual." So he *had* read the play. "Say, would you like to have a cup of coffee? Got this stuff from Tanganyika. Dynamite." Before Ian could answer, Brashford poured him a small cup from a silver pot he had on the table.

"I called him Ham to make the point." The coffee was as strong as it was down home. "Ham was cursed because he saw his father, Noah, naked. In *Reckless Eyeballing*, Ham Hill is cursed because he allegedly stared at a white woman too long."

"Cursed so that he will be black and elongated!"

"What?"

"That he be black and elongated. That's the curse, and when they said elongated they weren't talking about his arms either. It was the Talmud that laid the curse on Ham and us. Anyway, these white people don't care how smart you are or how impressive you are." Brashford rose and walked toward a window. He was the type of guy who couldn't keep still.

"Ball, they're pushing your play because—" Every black guy had a cynical theory about why another black guy was "successful."

"Because what?" Ian asked. Brashford was chuckling again. Ian looked at his smooth chin and cheeks. How did he remove all the hair from his face? It was completely bald. Brashford would attribute this to his Cherokee genes.

"Because you got that white woman's monologue in the play. The one about her and the lynched nigger being in the same boat. How are they going to be in the same boat? How are some white woman and a lynched castrated nigger going to be in the same boat? The reason you did that was because you wanted to make up with women for *Suzanna*. The one about the whore who takes on all of those guys in the fields. That was a brilliant play. Brilliant. You remember those fellowships I got you for that play, the awards." Brashford shook his head.

"I guess you're going to throw that up in my face forever."

Brashford swirled around. "Look, you little fuck—naw, skip it—"

"Go on. Tell me what's on your mind, old man!"

Brashford stared at him momentarily. "You guys don't know how hard it was back in the days when they had twilight zone–headed dudes wandering around New York hopped up on some kind of political bullshit and threatening guys like me who wrote the truth. Wrote it the way they saw it. It's like what Chester Himes said: 'All that matters now is to keep thinking the unthinkable and writing the unprintable and maybe I can break through this motherfucking race barrier that keeps us niggers suffocated.' And some of us believed that. Hell, if I'm writing articles about freedom all the time, and they bored with that, then let them be bored, because in the old African tales we came here with—the ones we knew before they took our brains to the cleaners—the god of drama demands that you tell the truth, and so lying is violating some sacred oath in a manner of speaking. So Chester and me, and some of the other guys, have stuck to our guns, but you guys and your generation, you've fallen victim to the moral laxity of the times. You ain't trickin' nobody. So since these broads have put a hurtin' on those four one-acters you've written since *Suzanna*, you plan to get yourself off the sex list by writing this pussy play. You're trying to get off the sex list. Admit it."

You should hear about how the fellas explain your success, old man, Ball started to say, but kept his peace. The reason that Chester Himes and Jake Brashford, and the others like them who risked their necks by trying to assert as large a range as their contemporaries, to break barriers, didn't get as far as some of the others, is because they were abrasive, went around with a chip on their shoulders. They were confrontational. Confrontation was passé. This was the eighties.

"What's wrong with you?" Brashford continued. "It's these white women who are carrying on the attack against black men today, because they struck a deal with white men who run the country. *You give us women the jobs, the opportunities, and we'll take the heat off of you and put it on Mose*, is the deal they struck. They have maneuvered these white boys who run the country, but they have to keep the persecution thing up in order to win new followers, and so they jump on po' Mose. They get Tremonisha and Johnnie Kranshaw to be their proxies in this attack. Sort of like the rich used to hire poor people to fight their wars. As for these Jewish women who are putting a hurtin' on black dudes in print—they know they can't change Abraham, Isaac, and Jacob, so they're rehearsing on us, and backing these literary sleep-in maids who are coming down on the brothers in a foul and horrendous manner. Now I don't approve of violence, but I can't help secretly applauding what that crazy dude did to Tremonisha." Ian looked at the wall above the Queen Anne sofa that Brashford sat on. There were framed portraits of Eugene O'Neill, and playbills from performances of O'Neill's plays. Jason Robards and Colleen Dewhurst dressed as O'Neill characters. Stills of scenes from *The Iceman Cometh*.

"How can you agree with what this guy did?" asked Ian. "You northern black intellectuals are always backing lunatics, just like you backed Idi Amin and Mark Essex. It's irresponsible if you ask me—you're always complaining, always feeling sorry for yourself—"

"You don't know the ropes, youngster." Brashford rose and walked to the front of his bookshelf. "Any black man, I don't care how much prominence he has, if he isn't bitter by the age of forty has lived his life as a fool. We can't get through the day without somebody inviting us outside. Going out on us. Gettin' it from every direction. White people, black people, faggots, Jews, Third World women, you name it. Some take to alcohol, some commit suicide; that is, if diabetes and cancer don't get them first. And homicide. All you hear on the media is stuff about white women getting assaulted. The movies are always about monsters from space, creatures from the deep, all with one thing on their mind: white women. Read all the Nazi books. All about saving white women. Well, according to statistics, being a white woman is the safest thing you can be. If you're a white woman your chances of being murdered is one in three hundred sixty-nine. If you're a white man, one in one thirty-one, if you're a black woman, one in one hundred four, but if you're a black man it's one in twenty-one. Get that? One in twenty-one. In other words, being Mose is the riskies' thing you can be. When you're born a black man you're taking your life into your hands. The brothers' killing of one another has become so epidemic that the phenomenon was written up in *Science* magazine. Living like a black man is like doing hand-to-hand combat every day of your life."

"But you're not in combat. You have this terrific studio, and I hear that your home on Long Island is a regular villa. Yet you're always going after somebody in print. Attacking people. Those nasty letters you write to *The New York Pillar*. I mean, put a piece of paper in your typewriter and all of a sudden it becomes a war zone."

Brashford shook his head. "You guys don't know how hard it was in the fifties. Nobody gave a damn about you unless you were writing some sensational, titillating play." You should know, Ball thought.

"Sure, I lucked up and got a hit. But that doesn't mean that I was supposed to relax after that. The play ran on Broadway and I invested the money. Everything that I have, I earned, but don't think that I don't know that to them I'm just another nigger. Listen, let me tell you a joke. A Jew, a Pole, and a black man arrive at the pearly gates and are told by Saint Peter that they can only enter the Kingdom if they spell a word. The Jew and the Pole are asked to spell God. They do so and are admitted. The black man is asked to spell chrysanthemum. It is always going to be twice as hard for us. In fact," Brashford continued, "I'm thinking about going into business. I don't want what happened to those Afro writers of the forties to happen to me. I'm going in the rent-a-male-chauvinist business."

"What?"

"Rent a male chauvinist. This will solve the unemployment problems of black men. See, some of these black feminists and the white ones who are backing them like Becky French have made the afro man into an international scapegoat. Man, you even got German, East Indian, and Japanese women writing things against black men in America, as if the men in their countries spend all of their time doing the dishes and changing diapers.

"So what I will do is rent out these black men. You know all those female vice-presidents and college professors who've sold out to white men for the androgynous god Mammon? They're not going to bite the hand that feeds them, so I will rent them black men they can cuss out and abuse. I would charge them a thousand dollars an hour. I would even have group rates. I would give discounts. I would send these black men all over the world, and let these liberated women in all of the countries kick these American black men in the ass for a fee. I would do quite a business, because everywhere these bitches' books and plays have gone, a hysteria has been built up against black men."

Ian Ball couldn't help laughing. No matter what he and the fellas thought about Brashford, nobody denied that he was funny. He could have made millions as a stand-up comedian, people were always saying.

"Anyway, here's your play." He walked to a table he said he'd bought in Italy, picked up his script, and threw it at Ball. "It's a good play except for that woman's monologue. Shit, a white woman was married to Robert E. Lee. There are white women in the Klan, and the Nazi party. I guess next you're going to write a play praising white women in the Nazi party, claiming that they, the niggers, and the Jews are in the same boat. That all of them are victims."

"It's being done. Becky French. She's producing a play about Eva Braun. It's about how Eva Braun was a victim."

"What?" Even Brashford's jaw dropped, he who let nothing excite him.

"Sure. In fact, she even tried to push me and Jim out of the Mountbatten so's she could put the play about Eva Braun in there."

"See. I told you these feminists, or whatever they're calling themselves, had lost their minds. What's the difference between them and the right wing? You see them down there on Times Square picketing against the pornographers. What's wrong with those women showing some tits and ass? And then they beatin' up on poor Mose 'cause he ain't got no job no pride no power no nothin', cannon fodder for their wars, scapegoat for their failures, a two-legged insurance policy and safety valve for America. I knew that it wouldn't be long before they'd be romanticizing some Nazi. You see, it's logic like Becky's that makes me and some of the other guys say that the women can't handle reason and ought to be put back in the kitchen."

"How's the new play coming?" It came out before he could catch himself. He merely wanted to change the subject, but knew that this would begin another misogynist tirade.

"Yeah. Well, you're not the only one asking me that. Directors. Producers. All callin' me for twenty-four years, ever since *The Man* . . . asking me where's the new play. Well, I'll tell you why I haven't finished the play. It's because the Jews have stolen all of the black material, so there's nothing for me to write about. Every time you turn on the TV or go to the movies or read a new play or novel, there's some Jewish writer, director, or producer who thinks that he knows more about niggers than they know about themselves, and who's cashing in on the need of Americans to consume the black style without having anything to do with niggers. Ralph Ellison was right. We're just a natural resource to them. Something that they can rip off. Their views of us haven't changed since the days of slavery."

"So if the Jews have stolen all of the black material, what are you going to write about?" Brashford looked at his watch.

"Armenians. I'm going to write about Armenians. I'm going to create characters with depth and nuance." He rose, went to the full-length mirror, and put on a tie. He went to the other end of the spacious room and removed a jacket from a closet.

It was velvet. Brashford wore suits and sports jackets, his shoes were always shined, and his hair trimmed. It was rumored that he'd had a drinking problem, but had been cured. (In the 1950s he'd gone around saying that in order to write like O'Neill, one had to live like O'Neill.) "I'm doing my research and I've been taking notes for about three years. I'm going to ask for complete control over this play, because you know some of these directors and producers and people will probably get upset about me writing about Armenians. Joyce can write about Jews, Updike, Malamud, and Wolfe can write about blacks, but when we try to write about something outside of the black experience, as they used to call it, we're accused of, well, like the title of your play, *Reckless Eyeballing*." Brashford pulled out his wallet and inspected his cash and cards. He spent a lot of time buying clothes and eating in fancy restaurants.

"I'm glad you liked something about my play," Ball said. Brashford walked over and touched Ian's shoulders.

"Look, Ian, I wouldn't have gotten you those fellowships and grants if I didn't think you had talent. You remember after the then incipient feminist movement got their contacts among the patrons to stop you, it was my contacts that kept you going. That *Suzanna* was a disaster, but I got them to give you that award."

"Sure came in handy."

"You see there. I mean I would have helped some of your other friends if they weren't so pushy. Said all of those mean things about me. That Randy Shank. Called me those names. Hear he's in bad shape. Cleaning restrooms or something. You can't get help from the people in this town with a hostile attitude." He was combing his hair as he said hostile. He had white hair and a white beard. He looked most distinguished.

"Look, I got to go," he said, looking at his watch. "Some German scholar is writing a book about my plays." *Plays?* Ball thought. "He and his wife are taking me to the opera. I think it's Wagner. Did you know that they used Wagner's music in the soundtrack of *The Birth of a Nation*, and that the Americans commissioned Wagner to write the music for the American Centennial? Man, these American and German Nazis were together even way back then in 1876. Anyway, I hope that it's not a whole lot of fat white people jumping up and down screaming and hollering at the top of their lungs." They laughed as they started out of the building. The white doorman greeted Brashford, but ignored Ian. He looked him up and down again. The doorman blew his whistle to get the attention of a cab driver.

"How are you going to bring it off? I mean, reading about Armenians is one thing, but writing about them—I don't know."

"I'll do it. You watch. The play is about a conflict between a broken-down alcoholic Armenian actor, his hophead wife, and their two loser sons."

"You talk about the Jews all the time. Why don't you write something about them?"

"Are you kiddin'? Did you see what they did to Chester Himes and Langston Hughes? By the time they finished with Zora Neale she was mopping floors. No. No. I'm not writing about no Jews. I'll stick to Armenians." A cab pulled up and the doorman opened the door for Brashford. He climbed into the backseat. Ian was standing at the curb.

"Good luck with the play. With that Jim Minsk directing the work it's bound to be a hit. He's a great director." The car pulled away before Ian could respond. He wanted to ask Brashford why he would praise Jim so when he knew that Jim was Jewish. How could Brashford have it both ways, put down Jews for an hour or so and then praise one? Brashford's stack of white hair showed above the taxi's backseat as the car disappeared into traffic.

7

Flying a plane these days was like playing Russian roulette; you never knew which one would have a pilot flying in bad weather just to make his schedule, or a pilot who was addicted to alcohol or drugs. Every time the plane Jim was aboard passed through dark clouds he felt as though he were riding a bucking horse. Finally he saw some lights below, and the fasten-your-seat-belt come on. The commuter plane landed.

The airport was small. Instead of a gate, the stairs for the passengers to descend upon were wheeled up. As he entered the terminal, he came upon a man with a gaunt, nearly skeletal face holding a sign: "Welcome, Jim Minsk." The man was lemon-colored and grinning.

"Mr. Minsk," he said, "it's an honor," extending his hand. Jim shook his hand and returned a smile.

"I'm glad to be on the ground. It was bumpy up there," Jim said.

"We've had some bad weather these last few days. Do you have any more bags?"

"Just a carry-on," Jim said, pointing to a black nylon garment bag. Inside the terminal there were pinball machines and video games lined up against the walls. Two commuter airlines shared the terminal's single counter. He walked over to the newsstand, Professor Michael Steepes, as the man had introduced himself, following. A man was brewing coffee. There were sandwiches for sale. Minsk approached the magazine rack. He noticed some cheap pulp magazine with articles about the Nazis. In fact, there were so many books, television shows, and movies about the Nazis, he was sure that it was difficult for the younger generation, who saw the swastika as some kind of toy, to determine who had really won the war. Roosevelt's name had become synonymous with welfarism; Winston Churchill's best speech had been adopted by a fast food commercial; Stalin had been de-Stalinized. Only Hitler fascinated the 1980s as much as he did the 1930s and 1940s. He must have been a charmer for Gertrude Stein to nominate him for a Nobel Peace Prize and for even Walter Lippmann to say nice things about him. One magazine carried a photo of Eva and Hitler talking. They both held their hands behind their backs. He was wearing a three-piece suit including knickers and a Tyrolean hat, and she was dressed in a style that might be called Aryan peasant. The headlines on the cover said: TEETH FOUND IN BUNKER NOT EVA'S.

He bought a copy of The New York Pillar, and some Life Savers. While waiting for his change he glanced at the leading news story. The Flower Phantom had struck again. This time his victim was a feminist revisionist who had written that all of the black men in the South who had been accused of rape were actually guilty, and had deserved to be lynched. The same M.O. had been used. The man had tied the woman and then began to recite her alleged crimes against black men. He left her a chrysanthemum. Sick.

"How far is Mary Phegan?" Minsk asked as he and his escort, the lanky Professor Steepes, walked out of the terminal.

"We should be there in an hour." They got into Professor Steepes' small station wagon and headed toward the highway. They passed miles of farmland on which grew pecan trees, apple trees, cotton, and soybeans, and occasionally he noticed some tobacco. About thirty miles from their destination, the full moon appeared. Down here it wasn't umbraged by man-made lights, and it gave the landscape an eerie and primitive slant. Steepes hadn't changed his expression. His grin seemed frozen. There was something about him that gave Jim the creeps.

"I'm looking forward to the play." He had been invited to Mary Phegan to be the celebrity spectator at an annual play that had been performed by the Mary Phegan drama department since 1912.

"We're looking forward to your seeing it," Steepes said, turning toward Minsk and grinning even wider. Minsk felt uneasy, and reached inside his trench coat for a cigarette. "Smoke?" he asked, turning to Steepes.

"No," Steepes said. Steepes turned on the radio. Static came blasting forth. "In local news, the F.B.I. was involved in a shoot-out with the members of Nebuchadnezzar Legions, a vigilante hate group that has declared war on what they describe as the Zionist Administration in Washington. A search of their trailer turned up antitank weapons, hand grenades, and machine guns. As they entered the courtroom, the shackled prisoners began shouting, 'Black Death Is Back,' and 'Crucify the Jews.'" Minsk felt Steepes edging a look at him out of the corner of his eye. Steepes turned to another station. They heard a frenetic voice. "Ah Sinful Nation!!! People laden with wickedness, evil race, corrupt children! That's not your preacher talking but the word of the Lord, brothers and sisters, the word of Gawwwwd. The Jews are the lost sheep of Israel, brothers and sisters. Bending down to No-Gods. The No-Gods of communism, atheism, marxism. The Jews and the blacks are the children of Satan, ladies and gentlemen, descendants of Cain." The preacher's comments were accompanied by enthusiastic shouts of a-men, and hallelujahs. "It was this nation of harlots, the Jews, who killed Jesus Christ, brothers and sisters. Killed him, because the Lord was on to these idolators. They hanged him and pierced his side."

"Would you turn that thing off," Jim finally requested. Jim

Minsk decided that he didn't like Michael Steepes. Finally, Minsk saw the campus of Mary Phegan looming on a mountain in the distance.

"Well, we're here," Steepes said. "Hope that we can make it as exciting for you as New York. We'll try. The last excitement we had around these parts was in 1912. A lynching. I'm sure that you heard about it," Steepes said with a nasty chuckle. It was wasted because Minsk had fallen asleep.

Professor Steepes and Jim Minsk walked from the parking lot toward the campus's main building. The architectural style was of the Paranoid School of the late 1880s, an austere fortress-styled building made of brick and equipped with a tower that one finds in parts of Ohio, Wisconsin, and Minnesota. There were two men standing at the top of the gray wooden steps. As they came closer to where the men stood, Jim saw the pair begin to smile. One man, wearing a three-piece suit and striped tie like Professor Steepes, stood with his hands behind his back. He had the slitted eyes and long, oval face of John Carradine. The other man was younger. He had red hair and a red beard, and eyes like a goat's. Outside of these two and Michael Steepes, who was carrying his bags, there were no other people around. Professor Steepes introduced them as James Watson, the tall man, and Thomas Rhodes, the medium-sized man with the red hair. Watson was the president, and Rhodes was the provost.

"I can't tell you how honored we are to have you here. I trust your trip down was satisfactory," Watson said, as they walked into the building. The two men were on either side of him; Steepes had gone to place his bags in the guest cottage the school reserved for visitors. The wooden floors were shiny and there was an old, elaborate staircase made of wrought iron that led to the other floors. Inside the president's office, Watson offered Minsk a drink. Mr. Rhodes went into another room to mix Minsk a martini. He brought the president some George Dickel sour mash whiskey, and Rhodes had a glass of the same for himself.

"Here's to your good health." The three raised their glasses in a toast. Minsk thought he noticed some ironic eye exchange between the two men when Watson said "good health." Rhodes noticed Minsk glancing at the portrait of Jesus Christ on the wall. The portrait painter had given Christ a sinister smile.

"We may be a Christian school, but we do enjoy some earthly vices from time to time. Not as strict as some of these other southern fundamentalists down here. Why, we have seminars on Tillich, Barth, and Heidegger," he said, taking a sip of whiskey.

"I heard one of the local preachers on the radio on the way here. The most hateful junk you've ever heard. A raving anti-Semite." The two men stared at each other for a few seconds, following Minsk's complaint.

"Throwbacks," Rhodes finally said. "They're still against the teaching of evolution." The three men laughed. "There are people down here who believe that the earth is flat and that if you fly too high you'll punch a hole in the sky. We're sort of an oasis of civilization within this cultural wasteland."

"The people in this neck of the woods have a yearning for the old populist values. William Jennings Bryan is still a big hero to them. You know what Mencken said about him," Watson said. The other men shook their heads.

"He said that people down here used his hair to cure gallstones." The three laughed. What urbane and civilized men these were, Minsk thought. He glanced at the bookshelves, which were stacked with books on philosophy, science, and religion. There were even some up-to-date novels.

"You're doing a play by Ian Ball, I hear," Rhodes said. "I like his stuff. He's quiet. Not like those mau maus who used to write that junk threatening white people. They've all disappeared. We have one here that we keep around for our amusement, though I will admit that some of his essays on the English Romantics are not bad, considering—"

"He's talking 'bout Steepes, Mr. Minsk," Watson said. "He's our resident mau mau. Capable fellow, but from time to time he wanders off into these cumbersome monologues about his blackness."

"Steepes, he's—"

"He's black, as they're calling themselves these days," Rhodes said.

"But, I thought—"

"You're not the first one to think that Steepes is white. We have a lot of blacks down here who have blond hair and blue eyes. We Southerners can detect them, though."

"He's a good man. Popular with the students. And he doesn't give us half the trouble of the blacks here in the States. Every time you turn around they're up in arms about something. Steepes is from Jamaica. The British somehow found a way to civilize them."

"So that explains the British accent," Minsk said.

"His most cherished possession is a photo of him bowing down to the queen," Rhodes said.

"Hear him tell it you'd think that he was Malcolm X and Marcus Garvey combined, but actually he's as harmless as a pail of milk," Watson said.

"He's always talking about the black community when the nearest black is about thirty miles from here." Watson and Rhodes laughed. Minsk was becoming annoyed at the direction their humor was taking, and when Watson got serious Minsk was relieved.

"Well, Mr. Minsk, I hope you'll have an enjoyable stay. Your presence will provide a needed shot in the arm to our fledgling drama program. Every year since 1912, the college has been performing this show. It's kind of like a tradition." The window slammed shut. The impact startled the three men. Rhodes got up and raised the window.

"What's the play about?" Minsk asked.

"Oh, it's hardly connected, just a series of scenes and sight gags. I guess it's our own brand of avant-garde theater, Mr. Minsk." Watson and Rhodes laughed, and once again exchanged telling glances.

"Yes, we've always tried to be up-to-date," Rhodes said. "Mr. Minsk, have you had dinner?"

"I had a meal on the plane," Minsk said. "It wasn't exactly the Chez Panisse." Watson looked at his watch.

"We'll have Mr. Rhodes escort you to your cottage. You have about an hour to relax and clean up. I'll come and get you after that." The three men rose.

"Mr. Minsk, you really don't know how grateful we are to have you down here. If there's anything I can do to make you comfortable, just say so." Minsk thanked Watson and followed Rhodes out of the room.

Rhodes and Minsk walked down a tree-lined path toward the guest cottage. The campus was quiet except for the chirping of crickets and the incessant warbling of night birds. It was cool. Minsk was glad to get out of New York, which was hot and muggy. Finally Rhodes, the man waddling alongside him, who probably took out after the carbohydrates between breakfast and lunch and dinner, said: "What's Ball's play all about?"

"It's about the lynching of a black lad down here for staring at a white woman. Only Ball has introduced a twist. He has the woman the kid allegedly stared at demand that his body be exhumed so that the corpse can be tried. She wants to erase any doubts in the public's mind that she was not the cause of the eyeballing she got." Both men laughed.

"That Ball is hilarious. He has a fantastic range."

"We thought that it was a fantasy at first, and then Ball produced an article that appeared in *Ebony* magazine regarding a Mississippi man who was actually arrested for what was called 'reckless eyeballing.'"

"We've changed since those times, Mr. Minsk. This is 'the New South.' The races get along fine down here. We don't lynch Negroes anymore." Minsk thought that the stress Rhodes placed on *Negroes* was peculiar. He glanced at the man's flat, vacuous face and decided that there was no malicious intent. He read everything but the man's goat eyes, which were difficult to examine; one couldn't determine whether they were staring at you or away from you. Rhodes left Minsk at the door of the small guest cottage. He told Minsk to call him at home if he had any difficulty. Minsk walked to the inside of the cottage. It was cozy. There was a fireplace and a couple of straight-back chairs with cane seats and a rocking chair. In the bedroom was a brass bed covered with an ancient quilt. Hanging over the bed was a picture of Jesus of Nazareth. He remembered what his crotchety father had said about Jesus when he was growing up. He called the rabbi from Galilee a magician and sorcerer.

9

When the three men entered the small stadium, the students were already there. This surprised Minsk because, though he had seen many cars parked in the parking lots, he hadn't seen any people, nor had he heard anybody while entering the stadium. The five hundred or so spectators sat in one section of the small stadium. The other sections were dark. The men wore suits and ties and the women wore white dresses. He looked around and all he could think about were the models on the boxes of soap, with their confident grins. He felt the energy of their eyes upon him so intensely that he nearly stumbled and had to be aided by Watson and Rhodes as they started down one of the aisles and toward the front row. In front of their seats a red, white, and blue banner had been hung, and at the far end of the stadium there stood a large white cross that was blinking yellow from the lightbulbs. Rhodes and Watson sat next to him. He looked about at the crowd, and they were all looking at him. He could see their faces behind the candles that each had lit. He asked for a program and was told that there was none.

"In keeping with tradition, nothing about the ceremony should be written down," Watson said.

"Ceremony? I thought you said it was a play."

"Semantics," Rhodes said and glanced at Minsk. Minsk didn't like the look.

The performance space was shaped like a ring. A man dressed like Count Dracula with his caped arm in front of his face stood at the center. This had to be some kind of joke, but nobody laughed. Dracula said, in a thick Romanian accent, "Blood. I've been vagabonding all over Europe pursuing my tastes. I'm tired of the blood of infidels. It doesn't have that tartness, that sizzle you have in Christian blood. Christian blood tastes carbonated, like cherry cola. I think that I'm going to shrivel up into dust if I don't get some soon." Another spotlight is cast upon a woman in a negligee lying on top of an oversized bed. Her arm dangles over the side. One hand holds a long-stemmed rose. A canopy hangs over the bed. "Ah, there," the actor playing Dracula says. "At last. I'll get a good day's sleep tomorrow." The count begins to creep toward the bed where the sleeping maiden is lying, her blond hair spread to each side of her head. As he bends down and is about to sink his fangs into the maiden's throat, she bolts.

"Get thee back, Jew, in the name of him whose precious blood was shed on Calvary." The students in the stadium affirmed her pleas with hallelujahs and a-mens. Minsk saw some of them, behind the candles, their eyes rolling about. Others raised their hands. It was at that point in "the play" that he began to examine his options for escape. The actress playing the Christian maiden was still carrying on, spilling out her words of Jew-loathing curses as the vampire began to sink, his eyes protuberant. The audience applauded as the performance area began to turn dark again, with only the outlines of the prop people setting up the next scene to be seen.

"What was the point of all of that—why did you bring me down here to see this anti-Semitic filth?" Minsk protested, only to be silenced by Watson, sitting next to him. In the next scene a caricature of a medieval Jew in a long, black robe and cap creeps onto the set, whose only prop is a wall from which hangs a picture of Madonna and child. The Jew looks both ways, plucks the painting from the wall with his long, sinister-looking fingers, and then hides it under his robe. At that point, a couple of bearded guys in urban cowboy clothes and good old boy caps come running into the area. They snatch the painting, and one of the good old boys twists the Jew's wrist, forcing him onto his knees. He slaps him.

"Don't put that evil eye on me, Jew," he says as he beats the actor playing the Jew. This delights the crowd. One of the good old boys begins to push a ham sandwich down the Jew's mouth and laughs as he gags. Another one hoses down the Jew. "How'd you like a little baptism, you kike?" he says, laughing.

"Look, I don't want to stay here and watch this shit. Take me back to the airport." But when Jim rose he felt something hard poking at his ribs. Rhodes had a pistol.

"Sit back down, you son of a bitch. You'll miss the best part." From the look in his eyes Minsk knew that there would be trouble ahead. There was something hurt, hateful, and wounded in Rhodes' eyes. There was fascination. The hatred had twisted his swinish face.

The only thoughts that Minsk had at that moment were about how to get out of the stadium. It had four exits that could be reached by walking up the aisle, but he didn't want to take the chance of having to run through a gauntlet of these clean Christians, who now seemed out for blood. He would have to leap over the railing in front of the seats and try to reach one of the tunnels located below the stands.

The stadium was lit again from the candles. The lights in the performance area came up. A black man in a dirty shirt and overalls stood in the spotlight. Some of the people in the audience began to weep. This must be the main part of the play, Minsk thought. He could hear his heart beat.

The character, Jim Conley, a janitor in Leo Frank's pencil factory, was being played by Michael Steepes, who'd been done up with black greasepaint and red lips. More people in the audience began to weep; as he began to speak his lines, a hush fell over the audience.

"I reckon I worked for Mr. Frank for a long time. Mr.

Frank was a nice, honorable man." (Some members of the audience hiss.) "Treated us nigras well, and wasn't as hard on us as some of the other white people I worked for, I reckon. He'd built his pencil factory into quite a business. Married high class.

"He was a real fambly man. So I thought. My mind about that was changed in a hurry. One Satiddy mo'nin' I was working. I never will forget it. I was sweeping the flo' and who should walk in but Mary Phegan. As fine a young woman as you want to meet." (People in the audience begin to sob. A second spotlight focuses upon an actress in white ballerina outfit with bridal headdress who begins to spin out to the performance area to the accompaniment of weepy and sad strings.) "She had such a pretty face, that Mary Phegan, kind of looked like Jesus' mother must have looked when she was a little girl. Pretty hair, blue eyes. She was like a sweet little bluebird. Everything about her was sweet." Minsk turned to Rhodes and then to Watson. They were staring at him, angrily. A woman in the audience rose, lifted her hands and screamed, "For shame, how could he. How could he have done it?" and she fainted and two women dressed as nurses rushed down the aisle to her aid. Minsk looked over his shoulder. It appeared that the whole audience was alternately staring from him to the play. He began to sweat. As soon as the ballerina disappeared, a medium-sized man with big eyes, well-groomed hair, wearing pants with a sharp crease, white and brown shoes, and a striped shirt with arm band came across the stadium toward the lighted area. He was carrying the girl in his arms. Debris began to rain down on the field. People began to shout and scream. Jim Conley, the character that Steepes was playing, turned to the man who was approaching. A soft drink can hit Minsk on the head. Rhodes turned to him. "Sorry about that." He began to laugh. (Steepes sees the man carrying the girl, drops his broom, and rotates his eyes.)

"Mr. Frank, where you going with . . . Mary Phegan?"

(With considerable agitation) "Look. It was an accident. You got to help me bury . . ."

"She dead, Mr. Frank? She dead?" The audience was now screaming, "Death to the Jews" and "Remember Mary Phegan." Minsk decided that it was now or never. He shot up from his seat and leaped over the railing. He began to run toward the opposite end of the field, toward one of the tunnels leading out of the stadium. He ran through the set, knocking over Steepes, the actor playing Leo Frank, and the girl that he was carrying. Steepes gave chase. Before he entered the tunnel Jim looked over his shoulder. People were rushing down the aisles and leaping over the railings. Midway through the tunnel he heard angry voices coming from the other end. He ran back into the stadium, only to see the mob heading toward him. There was a noticeable absence of brunettes among them. They were heading at him from all directions. Minsk started punching. A few of them fell but the others kept coming. He felt their hard blows upon his body until things went black. Before passing out he could hear them screaming, shrieking terrible and ugly things.

10

Ball had been drunk since he heard of Jim's death on the news. On the third day of his hangover he received a call from Becky that Jim's mutilated body had been found on some deserted road. Ian wasn't home and so she left a message on his answering service. She said that the voice on the service was "terribly annoying," and that she wanted to meet with him to make a decision about the future of his play *Reckless Eyeballing*. He arrived at the Lord Mountbatten about five minutes before his appointment. Becky's assistant Ickey, wearing a short-sleeved shirt and beige gabardine pants, his figure showing him to be losing his private Battle of the Bulge, told him to sit down and wait. Periodically, Ickey looked up at Ball and chuckled sarcastically. After Ball waited twenty minutes, Ickey finally said that Becky would see him. Ickey escorted him into the office. There were posters on the wall advertising *Wrong-Headed Man*, with a photo depicting the rogue at the top of the stairs, pounding his chest, grinning widely while his victim, the missionary, his wife, who lay at the bottom of the steps, sprawled and weeping. The caption underneath the photo read, "She Was His Slave in Love."

Today, Becky wore a P.O.W. haircut, khaki-colored blouse, and baggy pants. She was wearing red high heels. He thought of himself relaxing against a bedroom wall, a smile on his face, and arms supporting his head while she raised and lowered herself on his johnson, grunting and working hard as she tried to "earn" her orgasm, as Clarence Major would write. She wore some jewelry. Turquoise bracelets (fake). She had no lips, feline eyes. He sat down.

"Terrible about Jim," she said, studying him to get his reaction to her words. "He showed such promise." Promise, he thought. Jim was one of the best directors on the New York scene and here was this twat saying that he had "promise," Ian thought.

"I'm going to miss him. We were buddies," Ian said.

"We're still trying to piece together the details of this tragedy. We tried to get in touch with the college, Mary Phegan, but the Georgia operator said that there was no such college. Would you like to have some coffee?"

"I need some," he said. She went over to a table that stood

in front of a window. Outside, old wavers, new wavers, and future wavers; writers, poets, playwrights, and tourists could be seen strolling down Avenue A.

She had her back to him. "Cream and sugar?" I'd like to cream you, Ball thought. He wanted to go up behind her, rub a stiff erection against her ass, and cup her breasts with his hands. He could imagine her closing her eyes and her tongue sliding over the part where her lips would ordinarily be, but he thought differently. She had a reputation for being difficult to bed. Some had even said that no man's panzer division had ever crossed her tight Maginot Line. She poured the contents of a white thermos into a ceramic cup that had Lord Mountbatten's heraldic shield on it. She gave him a professional smile as she handed him the coffee.

"We still plan to do your play, of course; Jim's death won't change that. I mean, we wouldn't think of scratching a play that Jim had such interest in. We'd like to make one change."

"Change?"

"Yes," she said, sipping from her cup and lowering her eyelids. "We think that the play still has some rough edges, and so we'd like to move it from the Lord Mountbatten to the Queen Mother." She studied him as he formed his response. The Queen Mother didn't have good equipment. Lights were bad, the stage small, and the seats uncomfortable. There was a limited supply of dressing room space, and it seated only ninety-nine people. It didn't have the Mountbatten's prestige.

"We're going to give it a workshop, and, well, if anything comes of it, we'll perhaps—well, there might be some room at the Mountbatten next season." He rose. He was angry.

"A workshop?" He looked down at her. He saw her finger move to the button that would summon Mr. Ickey. "But, but, Jim thought that it was a major play. Deserving of the Mountbatten. I don't get it. A workshop!"

Becky's assistant Ickey had gotten his mocking smile from her. She sighed. "Look, Jim's dead. I also don't mind telling you that I was against doing your play, originally. It read like a first draft. I was only complying with Jim's request." Yeah, I know all about it, Ball thought. He brought in all of the grants. He wished that the Flower Phantom would get this bitch, but reproached himself for even entertaining such a thought.

"Well, how do you feel about it? Take it or leave it."

"I guess that the Queen Mother is better than nothing." He thought of all of the fellas who weren't even able to get that. You should be grateful, he heard his mother say.

"I'm glad that you see it our way," she said, more relaxed now. "You know, Ian, you're pretty good. You continue to write and maybe one day you'll be as good as Tremonisha Smarts, and I might tell you that Tremonisha and I feel that you've come a long way from that misogynistic piece of drivel *Suzanna* that all of the male critics applauded." She looked up. Her assistant was standing in the doorway. He wore a smirk. "Tremonisha is on the phone."

"Tell her I'll call her back," Becky said, glancing at her watch. Ball could take a hint.

"Jim said that you were thinking of doing a play about Eva Braun." She'd returned her attention to the papers on her desk and seemed annoyed that he was still in the room. Probably liked to fuck with the man on the bottom, Ball thought. Probably masturbated to ragas.

"You say something?" She was impatient.

"Yeah. Jim said that you were considering a play about Eva Braun."

"Oh, yes. *Eva's Honeymoon.* We're going to do it in the Mountbatten." His mind flashed to the plump blonde who wore her hair like the 1940s Claudette Colbert. She was usually romping about that place in the mountains that Hitler built. Playing with puppies and making home movies. She was always smiling. He thought of what Brashford would say. "Shit, a white woman was married to Hitler."

"God knows we've heard enough about what the men thought." She stared hostilely at Ball when she said *men*. "And that little k—Jewish girl, Anne Frank, she's almost discussed in this town as much as the Rosenbergs. So now, Eva will have a chance to tell her side. How she was victimized." This bitch is incredible, Ball thought.

"Victimized? I don't follow, Becky. I always thought that Eva Braun was a Nazi." She jumped to her feet. She was shaking, she was so full of rage. "Just like you men! You rehabilitate the Waffen S.S. because they're men. But Eva! No, Eva's a woman! She was an innocent bystander in conflict between Jewish and German men! All of those women, victims in a war of male ego." She took out a handkerchief and blew her nose. As she did, he thought of the newsreels showing the women crying into their handkerchiefs and squealing as Hitler's motorcade passed, their arms raised in Nazi salutes just like everybody else's. Women throwing flowers, screaming, breaking down, wanting to wrap their legs around the Führer's hips and party all night.

"Yeah. Well, I gotta be going. One thing." He needed some air.

"What is it?" she asked, stamping a foot impatiently.

"Who's going to direct my play now that Jim's gone?"

"Tremonisha Smarts. She's read your script and will be contacting you. She said that she's having problems with some of your female characters." Becky said all of this with her head buried in the papers.

"What?" he said. His legs felt weak.

"Tremonisha Smarts is directing your play. Now, I have a lot of work to do. I—" He turned around and walked out of the office. *She's having problems with some of your female characters.* The words, said with a mean, sarcastic smile, stayed in his mind as he stood momentarily outside her door. Soon he heard her voice behind the door. "Hello, Tremonisha. He just left." This was followed by a triumphant laugh. Ickey looked up at him and chuckled. He looked up at the portrait of Shakespeare. Even Shakespeare seemed to be smiling, mocking him. "Nigger," the bard seemed to be saying, "who do you think you are, trying to express yourself in English? Don't you know that English is white peoples' language?" He left the theater with Shakespeare's laughter ringing in his ears. Becky, Ickey, and Shakespeare all seemed to be laughing at him, their faces in a heavy-handed montage like in an old film. He left feeling like something that sticks to the soles of your feet and smells bad.

11

For some reason, Tremonisha wanted their meeting to take place at the Oyster Bar located in Grand Central Station on East Forty-second Street. The building's artwork was elaborate. It reminded him of Henry James' prose style. Excessive, equivocating. It contrasted with the modernist temple, the Pan-Am Building, that stood behind it. Tremonisha was about forty-five minutes late, which gave him an opportunity to read *The New York Pillar*. The Flower Phantom, as the man who assaulted Tremonisha Smarts was called, had struck again, this time tying up at gunpoint and shaving the head of a feminist writer who had suggested in a book that the typical rapist was a black man. The newspaper was calling the culprit a hair fetishist because of his practice of collecting the victim's hair and placing it in a black plastic bag. A sketch of the Flower

Phantom appeared in all of the newspapers. Panels of experts discussed him on television. Some black men began to appear in public wearing a chrysanthemum pinned to their clothes. Ian's head told him that this man was a lunatic who should be put away for a long time, but his gut was cheering the man on. His head was Dr. Jekyll, but his gut was Mr. Hyde.

The place was full of commuters who were gulping down oysters and crackers. Finally somebody said, "Mr. Ball." He looked up. She was standing there. Her skin was smooth and had a tapioca color. She wore a white turbanlike headpiece, earrings that dangled, bright red paint on her lips, which seemed in a puckered state. She wore black beads around her neck and the kind of skirt women wear in the Caribbean marketplace. She dressed like Carmen Miranda and had Carmen Miranda's sexy eyes.

"When they find that nigger I hope they put him under the jail." She sat down. "He walked about the room calling me a collaborator before he did it. Said that the French knew how to punish traitors."

"Brashford said that throughout history when the brothers feel that they're being pushed against the wall, they strike back and when they do strike back it's like a tornado, uprooting, flinging about, and dashing to pieces everything in its path. A tornado has no conscience. He says the fellas feel that they are catching it from all sides."

"What else would a senior male chauvinist like Brashford say? He's just a fifth-rate O'Neill anyway, and his opinions about women are just like O'Neill's. We're all whores to them. I'm really surprised that you seem to be agreeing with him." She went into her bag and removed a small gun. "I was always a pacifist, always sympathizing with these guys, but if one of them tries that again, I'm going to blow him away." Sympathize, Ball thought. By the end of *Wrong-Headed Man*, the lead villain has screwed his children, sodomized his missionary wife, put his mother-in-law in bondage, performed bestial acts with pets, and when the police break down the door he's emptied the fish bowl and is going after the fish.

"Get me a bowl of oyster stew and some crackers, and I think I'd like a bottle of Löwenbräu Light." She threw a hundred-dollar bill at him. As he rose to comply with her wish, a white man who could have been created by Sloan Wilson approached the table. He wore a blue three-piece suit without a trace of lint, black cordovan shoes, manicured nails. He was clean-shaven. As Ball started toward the order counter, he heard the man ask was she Tremonisha Smarts. He turned and she was signing the man's autograph and grinning. A European-American man came and took his order. He brought it back. "Isn't that Tremonisha Smarts sitting over there?" He told the man that it was, the man made a smart aleck grin like James Dean's, looked him up and down and said, no charge. "I loved that play," he said. He came back and set down the tray bearing Tre's requests and his shrimp cocktail.

She threw the script onto the table.

"I brought this script to you. I've red-penciled all of my suggestions; of course you'll have the final say so of what goes, and what's to be added. I think that the characters need more definition." She paused and stared into his eyes after that sentence. He looked away. "We're going to have to cut down on some of the props and costumes. Becky said they're reducing the original budget for the play."

"But Jim said that the budget was already skin and bones."

"Look, I just work here." You can say that again, Ball thought.

"Becky wants to put all of her money into Eva Braun's play. You ready for that? Now, I want you to take the script home and go over my corrections, I mean, my suggestions." You were right the first time, Ball thought. "And give me a call. We'll meet at my place early next week." She handed him her card.

12

The doorman at Tremonisha's apartment building was Randy
Shank, the first playwright who'd made the theater feminists'
sex list in the 1960s. The one who'd gotten into trouble with
his satire *The Rise and Fall of Mighty Joe Young*, whose prem-
ise was that American women craved to be raped by a beast.
The play not only caused problems for the author but for one
of the male critics who'd given it a good review. Feminists had
the man followed. The women who dated him were harassed
outside their apartment buildings by something calling itself
"the feminist education committee," whose members shouted
all kinds of rotten things about the critic as these women attempted to enter and leave their homes. The feminists ran-
sacked his office and smeared blood all over his typewriter and
papers. Ball was surprised to see Randy because he'd heard
that Randy had left for Europe. He'd heard rumors about
Randy and his travels through Amsterdam and Brussels. How
women waited for him in shifts at his favorite cafés. Shank was
stroking his chin and looking Ball up and down. He frowned
and folded his arms. He still walked with his shoulders stooped.
In his doorman's outfit he resembled a World War I Ukrainian
general.

"Randy, what are you doing here?" Ball asked.

"Well. It talks," he said, glowering. "You weren't so friendly
the other night. I caught you down in the East Village on

Avenue A. I called and you didn't even turn around to acknowledge me. And that woman you were with. She looked
like a bat out of hell. Had that next-wave shit all over her face
and one side of her hair dyed blond, the other looking like a
rooster had slept on it. What were you, high, or something?"

Funny line coming from a guy who in the sixties was so full
of heroin he couldn't stand up, Ian thought. "I don't know
what you're talking about," he said.

"It was Tuesday night, at about eleven A.M. down in the
Village. Avenue A. You walked right by me."

"I was working on my script Tuesday night; I didn't even
come out of the house."

"Well, if it wasn't you, somebody was wearing your face."
All of the fellas were saying that something had happened to
Shank in Europe. That there had been a personality change.
Maybe he was beginning to see apparitions.

"I thought you were in Europe," Ball said, hoping to steer
the conversation in a different direction.

"Oh, that. I got into a lot of hassles. Man, as soon as Tremonisha's plays and those other feminist bitches' books started to
get translated into foreign languages, the women in these
countries began to come down hard on black men. With the
missiles and the strong dollar, anti-Americanism is very rife."

"Look, I," Ball reached into his pocket.

"I don't need your money," Shank sneered. "I make enough
here. Got me a one-bedroom up on West End. I'm saving my
money and I'm going to stage my new play myself. That way
I'll have independence and won't have to rely on these downtown Jews to get my stuff over. I won't have to kiss anybody's
ass to get over."

Ball lifted the man from his feet. Ball may have been from
the South, but he knew about Afro-American signifying.
"What do you mean by that?" he said, ready to punch Shank.

"Nothing, man. I don't mean nothing." Ball let him down.

"Man, you country niggers are sure paranoid. Every time

somebody say something, you think they talking about you. I just be hearing things, that's all," he said, brushing himself off.

"Hearing what things?"

"Aw, man. You know there's always going to be talk. They say that you've given in to those dykes over there at the Mountbatten and that—" Shank covered his grin. "They say that now that the Jew boy, your security, has disappeared, Tremonisha"—he started to laugh aloud—"Tremonisha Smarts is directing your play." Shank doubled over, holding his gut, he was laughing so.

Ball thought for a moment. "So what's wrong with that?" Ball said, weakly. "She's a competent director."

"Aw, man, you know the reason the white boys love her so. It's because she portrays black men as hurried, inattentive lovers, and then there's that scene where this brute throws the woman down the stairs. They love that. That's all the white boys talk about. Man, do they cream behind that. They love stuff showing black dudes as animalistic sexual brutes because that's what they are. Just like when they called people cannibals. They're the biggest cannibals there are. They've cannibalized whole civilizations, they've cannibalized nature, they'd even cannibalize their own mothers." Ball had heard this speech a million times over the years in New York.

"I'm proud to have Tremonisha direct my play. I've learned a lot from her already."

"I agree with this Flower Phantom dude. He's right. Some of these black feminist writers are just as guilty as those French whores who collaborated with the Nazis. They deserve what they get. Cut off their hair, but leave a flower." He snapped his fingers, annoyed with himself. "Damn. Why didn't I think of that?" He stamped a foot.

"She's a collaborator because she told that columnist that rapists should be castrated. You know who's going to be castrated, don't you? Me and the fellas are going to contribute to this guy's defense fund if he's ever arrested. These Jew bitches are the ones behind it. They're putting Coretha and Clotel up to it. The way I figure, by having your play produced by Becky French, you're collaborating with these Zionists."

"Becky's not Jewish. Her family's ancestry goes all the way back to the *Mayflower*."

"That's what all these Jews say. They'd rather be pilgrims and the descendents of slave owners than be themselves. The Jews over here ain't the real Jews anyway."

Ball was looking toward the elevator in hopes of escaping Shank's crazy tirade. He wished that there was some way he could get away. He'd finally run into a man who was more extreme than Brashford in his anti-Semitism.

"How are these hymies over here supposed to be Jews when Abraham was a black man who fucked black women and had babies by them? The Flower Phantom, he said he'd get Becky French for agreeing with Tremonisha. Boy, why can't I be him." Shank had a reputation for being on the tail end of trends. Some people called him a copycat. Ball was becoming uncomfortable.

"Just like the Jew. Black people invented Judaism and then these Europeans take it over and water it down into some kind of stale crossover religion. Next the white Jews say they the only Jews and the original Jews, the black Jews who invented the religion in the first place, have to take a test when they go to Israel. Imagine that. Like these Falashas, whose traditions are pre-Talmudistic, have to take a test from these fake Jews when they go to Israel, and Israel is becoming such a theocratic state that they're even going to stop admitting these jive American Jews. These American Jews want it both ways. They play Marrano pretending to be Christian on the side, but in the back they still Jews. You heard what old Begin told them, didn't you? He said if they were so Jewish why don't they go to Israel, but now these reform Jews are scared because the Israeli people might even stop letting them in." Ball tried to sneak up to the elevator when the downstairs phone rang, but it stopped ringing and Shank continued. "The Jew hates the Gentile. He thinks that the Gentile is a dog, which explains why the Jews who own the media are always shoving this eye dog food up into his face. If you want to know how much the Jew hates the Gentile, watch the fall preview of TV shows, the movies that come out of Hollywood. He thinks the Gentile drinks too much and is uncivilized." Ball was relieved when a man dressed in a tweed jacket, brown gabardine pants, and casual shoes entered the lobby. The man's face was distinguished. He had a prominent nose. What in the old days the fellas would have called a "handsome" woman accompanied him. She was wearing a tweed jacket and conservatively styled British skirt, as well as a Robin Hood hat with a feather.

"How are you, Randy," she asked. Randy Shank turned to the couple.

"Oh, Mr. and Mrs. Epstein," he said gushingly, almost falling over himself, "shall I fetch you a taxi?" The woman nodded. With one eye shut she examined Ball. "Aren't you—yes, you are Ian Ball. I recognized your picture from the newspaper. Congratulations on your new play. Tragic about Jim Minsk," she said, shaking her head. "He was such a brilliant director." Randy Shank glanced from Mrs. Epstein to Ian Ball. He was angry. He couldn't stand it. Rage bristled at his insides.

"He went south to be the guest of some college. We can't even locate the college to find out what happened. We're going ahead anyway. You know, the show must go on. They've brought in Tremonisha Smarts to take his place," Ball said.

"Tremendous talent. Tremendous talent," Mr. Epstein said. "There's that one scene . . ." He trailed off and returned to sleeping on his feet.

"Well, good luck on your play," Mrs. Epstein said, smiling as she followed Shank outside. As the elevator shut behind him, Ball could hear Shank's whistle.

The door was open, but he knocked anyway. He heard

Tremonisha's voice, "Come in." He walked into the apartment. Tremonisha was on the phone, pacing up and down,
while puffing from the cigarette. She beckoned him to sit in a
chair. He sat down. The ambience of the apartment indicated
that she was in the upper range of the income distribution. He
recognized some paintings and prints by some of the leading
black Lower East Side painters. "You could have told me, you
still could have told me," she said to the person on the other
end. She was wearing some kind of designer pants with large
pockets, a blue blouse. She wore a blue kerchief on her head.
She was jangling as usual. Bracelets on her wrists and ankles.
"Shit on that, you still could have said something about it
before I read it in the papers. And what's this about my acting
surly? You said that about me. You know you did. Gal, I'm
not your fucking gal, don't give me that gal shit." She hung
up. She folded her arms and looked at him. "Men," she said.
He was embarrassed. He glanced toward the table. *The New
York Pillar*, 'MONISHA THROWS TANTRUM. A reporter was
quoting Towers Bradhurst, producer of the movie version of
Wrong-Headed Man, as saying that when Tremonisha Smarts,
the black playwright, was told that a white male screenwriter
had been hired to "doctor" her screenplay for the movie, Ms.
Smarts began throwing ashtrays and furniture in the producer's
office and when she finished the place looked as though the
Oakland Raiders had had a training session in there.

"Is anything wrong?"

"Is anything wrong, the nigger says," she mumbles. "No,
everything is just wonderful," she said, her voice coated with
sarcasm. "I need a drink." She went to the cabinet and removed a bottle of whiskey. She poured herself a large glass.
She gulped down some pills. She offered him some. He declined.

"They follow me out to Hollywood only to tell me that my
script wasn't adequate for my movie and so they brought
in_____." (She mentioned the name of a white male screen-

writer who'd been called the Charlie Parker of prose for his "be-bop style." The fellas had said that if he was the Charlie Parker of prose then Connie Francis was the princess of rock and roll.) She sat down, spread her legs, and leaned forward.

"I knew something was wrong with him. Every time we were supposed to have a script session he would get all tooted up and start talking about how black boys, as he called them, used to beat him at basketball and about how little he was. He wanted to know whether all the unsavory things that happened to the missionary in *Wrong-Headed Man* had really happened to me. What a voyeur."

Ball changed the subject. "Have you seen rehearsals for the important play, I mean the play about Eva Braun?" he asked.

"That silly thing," she said, throwing back her head. "Becky's still on the white woman as a victim trip. She feels that whatever evil white women do is traceable to some man. That's why she removed the white women from the lynching scene in your play."

"She what!" Ball said.

"Oh, didn't you know? She said that you and what's-his-name—"

"Jim."

"Right, Jim. She said that you and Jim had agreed."

"I certainly didn't, and Jim's not here."

"She feels that the white women who attended those lynchings did so under coercion by their husbands."

"They could have fooled me. I got those pictures up at the Schomburg. Their eyes are glassy and they wear fixed grins as they watch these poor men dangling from a rope. Drooling over the burnt flesh. I mean, some of them dragged their kids along. She's saying that they were pretending? Couldn't they have gotten baby-sitters?"

"She has the same theory about Nazi Germany. She said that Jewish and German women were innocent victims, caught in a battle between men over sexual turf. That the reason Jewish men got into trouble in Germany was because they couldn't get goyim ass off their minds. They were sexually addicted to white women. She got the idea from this film called *Jud Süss*. Afterward, during an interview, she said that if someone wrote a play about Nazi Germany from Eva Braun's point of view she would consider producing it. Mysteriously, a script turned up. It was written by some old biddy who lives in seclusion on Long Island."

"Yeah. She told me. That's why I got booted out of the Lord Mountbatten. You say she got the idea from a film?"

"She started to collect all kinds of supporting material. I've never seen her so driven. She collected cartoons from Nazi magazines and newspapers that showed Jewish men mugging and raping German women. The Jewish men were always drawn dark. But her main inspiration was the Nazi film. Becky saw it about thirty times."

"I've never heard of it."

"It rarely plays here in the States. We saw it at one of those bohemian art theaters in the village. You see, the Nazis were paranoid about Jewish men and foreigners diddling their women. It drove Joseph Goebbels crazy. He was the one behind the film. They'd play this movie for German troops before they went to the front. It would get them all steamed up. Some say that Goebbels arranged the film to get Hitler mad. They were always teasing Hitler about the grandfather on his father's side. Some bourgeois Jewish man impregnated his grandmother, a German who worked in his household. So in the film you have this usurious and dark Jew raping this German girl who goes through the film posing as some kind of idealized Gretel. In pigtails. Some say that this hatred of Jews by German men was the reason for the concentration camps. That's where Becky got the idea. That the World War Two holocaust was caused by a primal struggle between the Nordic man and the Moorish types."

"I've never heard that before; I thought they sent the Jews to those camps because they were scapegoats."

"Not a scapegoat. A scapegoat is one who is sacrificed to achieve a larger end. In Germany, the annihilation of the Jews was the end."

"What about this thing about the Jews killing Christ?"

"The Germans did it. The Romans brought in these German toughs to deal with the Jews just like they used to import southern cops to deal with niggers."

"You mean the Germans did it all along? Then they blame it on the Jews?"

"No longer; the Catholic Church is slowly absolving the Jews of the responsibility for Christ's murder. Pretty soon they'll probably blame it on us." She put her hand down her back for a moment and scratched. As she did this her ass shifted on the sofa's pillow. He didn't know anybody who had fucked her, but he could look at her and know that she was a gasper. One of those kind who took short breaths when you gave it to her hot.

"Anyway. This is where Becky got the idea. It's a white feminist bourgeois notion that women are innocent victims in a struggle between men."

"But I've heard you say the same thing. You said that the fight in this country is between black men and white men and that women are caught in the crossfire."

She jumped up from the sofa and started screaming. "That's a lie. I didn't say it."

"You did, you know you did," he persisted.

"That's a big lie, I never said it."

"Well, what about the castration thing? What about that?"

Ball caught himself. If he wanted to get his play done he could not alienate her. "Of course, I can see how you could be misquoted." She stood for a minute. She then sat down and lit a cigarette. "I never said it. Becky said it. As though she cared about the Jews. Sometimes she sounds like Henry Ford, she hates Jews so much. She concedes that their men are good lovers. She said that she experimented in college. That's why it's easy for her to say that the women had nothing to do with the rise of Hitler. As for Jewesses, as she calls them, she's always putting them down. Says they talk loud in restaurants and say crass and impolite things, always butting into people's business and always talking about money. She's always talking about their putting on too much makeup. She and her friends make fun of Jewish women getting nose operations."

"What?"

"Sure, didn't you know? Many Jewish women have nose operations to avoid looking 'Mediterranean.' They used to not be able to get jobs in Hollywood because they looked too 'Mediterranean.'"

"But I thought that the Jews owned the media. That's what Brashford says."

"They don't own the media, they own him."

"Man, do you get a kick out of running down black men?" This time his mother appeared in his mind's eye. She was wearing that bandanna on her head tied up in that certain way. "But on the other hand," he said before her frown appeared, "a lot of them deserve it." He swallowed bitter. Things were so tight for black men, here he was asking Tremonisha Smarts for a handout, in spite of all the things he and the fellas said about *Wrong-Headed Man* and her friends.

"They don't let Jews up there in the boardrooms of the big companies. They may have a few management positions, or they may be storekeepers, or speculate for the big capitalists, but they know that these capitalists will sell them out as they did in all the other countries. Some Jews try to cultivate an arrangement for protection, but others see the futility of it and remain separate.

"But back to the film. It's about this Jew named Joseph Ben Isaacher Oppenheimer. You see, he has this decadent duke in his debt and he strings the slob out in order to win political and sexual concessions for the other Jews. Like, he gets the duke to permit his people to enter Stuttgart from outside the town, where they're living in these filthy camps, and as the

Jews enter the German men cry out, 'What will happen to our wives and our daughters?' The Jews grin at the fräuleins with the same concupiscent stare that the black legislators in *The Birth of a Nation* have in that scene where they check out the southern belles in the legislature's gallery.

"In fact, the films *The Birth of a Nation* and *Jud Süss* have a lot in common. Just as *The Birth of a Nation* was innovative, the Nazis recruited some of Germany's supreme talent to appear in the film. It was directed by Harlan Veidt.

"The Jew even pimps for the duke. For example, there's one scene where the duke fantasizes about having some ballerinas perform for him and then, presto, in a cut we see the ballerinas the Jew has procured for the duke. Well, there's this one Aryan fräulein that the Jew really has the hots for. He finally rapes her, well, you don't see her actually raped, you see the Jew wrestling on the bed with her and then in the next scene she's walking down a road, defiled, ruined. She commits suicide and after the duke dies, depriving the Jew of his protection, the Jew is hanged for violating the old German law that forbade any Jew from having carnal knowledge of a Christian on penalty of being 'hanged for all to see.'

"Would you like to have some more coffee?" she asked, noticing that his cup was empty. Before he answered she had bounded into the kitchen. He had been trying his luck in the North since 1979 but still hadn't gotten used to the coffee. It was weak and people drank it with lots of milk. He always looked forward to going home to relax after he'd finished a project. They had real coffee there. She returned to the couch after pouring him some more.

"Boy, Becky has come a long way," she said. "She started out as a silly radical feminist and now she's producing a play that's sympathetic to Eva Braun, a Nazi. How people change. Seems that the left all over the West is going to the right. Wouldn't even be surprised if the Soviet Union got into a consumer binge. It always takes them a number of years to catch up with western fashion. How these radicals have changed."

Brashford said the same thing about you: Ball had the words right on the edge of his lips. A long time ago she wrote poems about blacks robbing department stores and shooting down the police, but recently she'd received a lot of criticism for traveling to South Africa. He decided to talk about something else.

"Eva Braun. Wasn't she that woman in the black bathing suit who was always romping about playing with puppies and pinching children on the cheeks at that place Hitler kept as a retreat?"

"Berchtesgaden," she said.

"Say, you really know a lot about it."

"I was doing research for this TV special. You know, the one I wrote about Jo Baker and Bessie Smith. Well, I ran across some kind of mention that Jo Baker had dinner with Hermann Göring; this huge Nazi whose abdomen was much wider than his hips, he tried to poison her."

Göring had a perpetual idiotic grin on his face, Ian remembered. He thought of the photos he'd seen of the fat buffoon in his cream-colored uniforms and giant raincoats. His big cheeks, tiny eyes, and helmet that fitted his head like a bucket. "Why?"

"The Nazis wanted to get rid of her because she was spying for the French and that's not all. I discovered that the night of his Austrian triumph Adolf Hitler slept in a bed with a picture of Josephine Baker hanging above the head. You know, Hitler hated jazz and was always scolding Eva about her collection of American jazz records. So why didn't he order Josephine Baker's picture to be removed from the wall of the inn where he slept that night? He was getting even with his mother. He had her picture on the wall of his bedroom, but the night that he's away from his room, sort of a shrine to his mother, he fantasizes about sleeping with the demon princess, the wild temptress Lilith, Erzulie, the flapper who brought jazz dance to the Folies. It was very significant that he had this fantasy in the land of his birth.

"Jesus Christ had the same experience with a prostitute on the road, away from his prying mother, whom some say was the prostitute. A Lilith or Erzulie of her time. He had the same problem. Jesus, Hitler, both had weak fathers and strong, manipulative mothers. He would have this ambivalent attitude toward the other women in his life, and finally toward the German nation, which in Nazi portraits is a prodigious butt buxom Brünhilde type blond blue-eyed white woman who is either holding a banner or a flag and at the lead of a vigilante mob. Hitler had the best ass in Germany available to him. Actresses, intellectuals, oxenlike bombshells, models, anything a man would desire, but he was a freak for these high-strung difficult types. That first one was his niece. It's rumored that she went and got pregnant by a Jew. Hitler was part Jewish. His relatives in London always threatened to tell the whole story. Hitler had to pay money to keep them quiet."

"Tremonisha, are you saying that World War Two happened because Hitler was trying to pass for white?"

"Overzealous assimilation, it happens all the time.

"Becky is wrong about the German women. When he pulled up to a station the women in the town would line up for a chance to sit in his lap for a couple of minutes. He was their pimp. He told them to give him babies and they did, and those babies died in Russia and France. They're just like these white women over here. Allow themselves to get sweet-talked and seduced. Look at all of the white women who voted for this war-monger and apartheid champion, Reagan. That's why Becky's wrong." Apartheid? Ian thought. Tre gave lectures at Women's Centers where no men were allowed. What about that apartheid?

She paused for a moment and drank from the glass.

"I think your version of what happened in Nazi Germany is far superior to Becky's," he said, trying to stay on her good side.

"Becky's not too much of an intellectual. I think that she went to school in California. But she's a go-getter all right.

Sure, Jim's genius brought in the grants, but Becky's administrative abilities kept the Lord Mountbatten in the black."

"How do you suppose that Jim's disappearance will affect his operation?"

"She didn't care about him. Thought he was arrogant. She just used him to pull in Jewish contributions, but now I understand that this lady in Long Island is going to pay some of the bills they used to pay."

He noticed her knee bobbing. "Did you know that the doorman downstairs is Randy Shank?"

She was shocked. Her eyes became gleeful. "I thought he looked familiar. Isn't that the nigger who used to dress up like Tom Mix and entertain tourists down in the Village during the fifties? Rent-a-nigger. A dollar a nigger?"

"Yes. He rented himself out to parties for a dollar. But you have to understand it was hard for black writers in those days, Brashford says. Randy played bongo drums in Washington Square Park during the day, and wrote at night. He paved the way for all of us." She covered her mouth and began to laugh. He looked around at her Danish furniture, blond tables, and lacquered black chairs. Her desk with the post-modernistic lamp. He looked at the original Afro-American paintings on the wall. Even with this affluent apartment, her money and fame, she was making fun of the brother while he was down.

"I thought he said that he was never going to return to America." She laughed some more.

"He's really bitter," Ball said. "He blames you and Becky for what happened to his career. Said Becky rejected his play for political reasons and that he had to leave Europe because as soon as your play and Johnnie Kranshaw's books started to get translated into foreign languages the women in those countries began to hate black American men, as if they didn't have enough problems. Says you even have women in Sri Lanka mad at them." She started to laugh. He wanted to grab her and shake her to make her stop laughing. It was a laugh of revenge, of hatred.

He left her that way and headed to the lobby. Shank was sitting at his doorman's desk reading a newspaper. He saw Ball and jumped up.

"Getting back to our conversation about the Jews." Oh, no, not again, Ball thought. "There's really no such thing as a white Jew. Real white people call Jews and the Arabs sand niggers behind their backs. Back in the 1900s and 1910s in this town they called the Russian ones Asiatics and Orientals. You couldn't pick up a paper in those days without reading about some Jewish pickpocket or pimp, and when they weren't doing that they were committing arson and poisoning horses." Ball tried to move out of the building, but Randy Shank blocked his way, insistent that he hear his tortured and odd theories. "They let them be white now because they serve the white man by keeping an eye on us, monitoring us, providing him with statistics about us, and interpreting us to the white man. The white man don't care about them. They didn't care if they burned up in the ovens, Roosevelt, Churchill, these American Jews even, nobody gave a damn. In the old days they even passed immigration laws to keep them out of the country."

Ball pushed him out of the way as the author of a collection of poems entitled *My Secret Enemy: Me* shouted at him, "THE JEWS! THE JEWS!" He was screaming. Randy followed Ball to the outside of the building, where Ball hailed a taxi. "Yeah, you fast all right, fast like you told us a long time ago, Ball, but I didn't know that you were that fast, that you would side with these bitches, these collaborators who are aiding our enemies in destroying us." Three or four cabs passed by. "You've broken ranks. They've made you into some kind of feminist." One pulled up. Ball jumped in. "They've made you into some kind of girl." Ball started to get out of the cab and kick his ass, but he had more important things to do. The cab leaped forward.

13

One night Ian was having plot problems, so he sauntered on over to Tre's, as he was beginning to call her. Randy Shank grumbled something as he walked in, perhaps still smarting over their last encounter. He went up to the elevator. As he approached Tre's apartment he heard somebody going upside somebody's head. He rushed to the door. It was open. He ran in and inside, a thin, wide bubble-eyed–looking man had Tre over the sofa's back and was strangling her. Ball grabbed the guy and threw him against the wall. The guy begged off. He was a wretched sight. He seemed to have slept in his clothes and his hair was wild and crazy, and he had on some weird clothes and shoes. Must be a musician, Ball thought. Then he recognized him. It was Dred Creme, the alto sax man. He was recently the subject of a long, difficult-to-read piece in one of the downtown art journals. He'd heard that Tre and Dred were tight. The only word the guy seemed to be sure of was "bitch."

"Hero. A hero." Dred started to reel and clap sarcastically. He could tell that the guy was high on something. To her he said, "I'm coming back later or I'll see you on the street. And when I finish with you you'll think that what that Flower Phantom did was mild." He staggered out of the apartment, but not before pausing to look Ball up and down. Ball matched him eyeball to eyeball. After Dred left, she walked up and put her arms around Ball's neck. He could feel her protuberances and her crevices. He wanted to gently let her down and gingerly fuck her on the couch right there, but then he decided that he didn't want to mix drama with sex. She finally let him go and sat down. He went over and sat on the sofa.

"He's always up here asking me for money to . . . to score with. He's snorted so much that he has to have surgery on his nose."

"Mind if I ask you something?"

"No," she said, "what is it? First, let me fix you a drink."

"I'll have grapefruit juice," Ball said. She went into the kitchen. He heard the mixer going. He heard her pouring the drinks. He looked at the coffee table, which had been moved to the side because of the struggle. On top was a book entitled *The Complete Works of Amy Lowell*, and next to that was a biography of Jane Austen, and knocked to the floor by the struggle, pages open, was Zora Neale Hurston's *Their Eyes Were Watching God*. Zora Neale Hurston wasn't a joiner but Tremonisha and others had claimed her as one of their own (though being middle-class Christian women at heart they wouldn't touch the Vodoun parts). They had joined Zora and joined her until she was all joined up. He picked the book up. She brought the tray back in and set it down on the table. They began to sip from the glasses.

"What did you want to ask me?" she asked.

"Well, if I may be frank, why do middle-class women like you go out with guys who want to beat you up and take your money?" He and the fellas always wondered why the musicians got all of the pussy. They concluded that it was because they did all of their talking with their instruments. They were nonverbal and so the bitches could run their mouths without fear of being interrupted or being called on the bullshit they were laying down. They also had theories about what the mouthpieces were substitutes for.

"It's none of your business," she said.

"These guys beat you up. Why don't you date somebody from your own class?"

"Leave." She pointed to the door. She ah . . . looked . . .

well, cute when she got mad. His mother's image appeared in his mind. She was giving him a stern look. He'd have to cool it. He wasn't as close to any woman as he was to his mother. Mama's boy? Why not. Ten years ago, when Freud was still riding high, you couldn't say that, but now that even some of his staunchest supporters were stating publicly that there was no empirical foundation whatsoever for his theories, you could say that you dug your mother without anybody, you know, looking at you funny. He started for the door. She'd gone to the couch and was sobbing on her arm. No. He decided. He'd have this out. "And another thing." She had her knees up, and he could see some of that excellent area above her knees: Her thighs were calling out to him, Ian, Ian, they were saying. He felt like pulling a Clark Gable, in that scene from *Gone With the Wind*, taking her into his arms—she beating his chest and kicking— and going into the bedroom to comfort her and stuff. But since he had her attention he decided to go for broke.

"I know I'm from the South, and I'm not all that hip to the way northern urban proletariat people talk, but some of the fellas say that they can't follow the dialect in *Wrong-Headed Man*. I mean, if they can't follow it, how are these white women who praise it so enthusiastically able to follow it! What do they know that the people who grew up actually speaking this language don't know? The fellas say—"

"What do those hardheaded fools say about me?"

"They say that you know as much about the way black people talk as Al Capp knew about Indian languages—" She started screaming and shouting. Then she started throwing things. He got out of there fast. He knew that he'd fucked up this time. Randy Shank was in the lobby, sitting at his desk. He was a little drunk.

"How come she let you up there and won't let none of the other fellas in there? Only people I see going up there are broads. Man, some of those chicks look rough. They could have gone into the wrestling business. I'll bet you're working on more than that play up there. Does she stopwatch the fore-

play? I'll bet a cold biddy like that times her sexual orgasms."
He then began to ramble.

"That Becky French fucked over my play. I'll fix her. That
Flower Phantom. That dude is right. Why didn't I think of
that?"

Ball started to punch out Shank. These northern guys were
always pushing him. He was always having to invite them outside. Always fucking with him. He was just about around the
corner from Tre's building when Shank came running out.

"The bitch wants to talk to you."

Randy Shank waited for him to come into the lobby. He
handed him the downstairs phone. He had a silly mocking
grin. Ball grabbed the phone from the sucker.

"Yes," he said. Randy was trying to listen, peering over the
top of the newspaper he pretended to be reading. Headlines
read: FLOWER PHANTOM'S NEW VICTIM.

"I don't want our . . . what just happened to come between
us and the play. We have to forget about our differences and
think of the play. I guess I lost my head. Throwing those
things at you like that. We'll work tomorrow." He noticed
Shank trying to spy. He put his hand over the receiver.

"Very well." He didn't want to let on how relieved he was.

They'd been working from four to eight P.M. She had
smoked a pack of cigarettes. When he went to the bathroom
during a break he noticed a lot of stress pills in her medicine

cabinet. Their exchanges since the argument had been cordial, civilized. A word she used a lot. This or that is so civilized, she'd say.

She knew her business. He had a tendency to tell rather than show, and she was teaching him the art of description. The art of movement. The art of character differentiation. She had recommended some minor changes in the script, having mostly to do with his tendency toward lengthy dialogue (Brashford's influence). Some of his lines had to be snipped. He had a tendency toward the robust, having grown up under a big sky. A sky uncluttered by skyscrapers and other attempts to "make order from chaos." He'd read that she had received a Phi Beta Kappa from a school in New York somewhere. The school where she met Becky. She'd had her stuff produced in a lot of workshops before hitting the big time with *Wrong-Headed Man*, which had become an international hit. One of the posters hanging in her living room showed a scene from *Wrong-Headed Man*, a black man with the missionary held over his head. He wears an idiotic grin. The viewer was provided with a good look at the missionary's thighs and bosom. He seems to be handling her with his big, hairy fists as easily as one would hold a doll.

The doorbell rang. She opened it to a white man. He was breathing hard. Sweating. She escorted him into the room.

"This is Detective Lawrence O'Reedy of the New York Police Department," she said proudly. The handshake was polite.

"He's trying to find the man who cut my hair."

"A hair fetishist," O'Reedy said, frowning at Ball.

"A hair fetishist? I thought the newspaper said that he cut off her hair because of World War Two, or something," Ball said. Tremonisha glared at him. O'Reedy ignored him.

"I came over to show you the profile of the man. It's based on your description of his face." She looked at the photo and then to Ball, who averted his eyes. There was a silence.

"Doesn't look like him at all," she said. "He's heavier in the face. Like Ball here." Detective O'Reedy stared at Ball. Ball squirmed in his chair.

"We'll do another sketch," Detective O'Reedy said.

"Since he was wearing a mask, we can only approximate his features." He studied Ball. Like Clint Eastwood, his idol, Detective O'Reedy talked with his face.

"Ball is working on a play. I'm helping him improve it. I'm making some minor changes."

"Playwright, huh?"

"Yes. Yes, sir," Ball said.

"Well, I have to be going," he said.

"Thanks for all you're doing," Tremonisha said, escorting him to the door.

Ball heard them talking low as they approached the door in the hall. Almost in a whisper. They talked that way for about three minutes. He heard the door shut. She returned to him. It was getting dark and he could see the moon beginning to appear over the East River. He was putting on his coat to leave. Their eyes met. They were that way for a long time. He could see her grunting and groaning as he moved his hips under her body. He wondered was she thinking the same thing. Probably not. She finally said it. He wondered what took her so long.

"You got a thing about black women. They're either vamps or being subservient to some man." She stressed *man*. "And then you give the old whorish white bitches in your play all the good lines, and don't leave no good lines for the sisters. I know all about your problem."

"What do you want me to do, Tre?" he said, eager to mend his ways.

"I want you to do better." She blew some smoke from the cigarette she held.

"I'll certainly work on it." Outside he waited for the elevator. He was stunned at what she was saying about white

women. Calling them whores and things. Making fun of
Becky. The white women made her. They produced her.
They promoted her plays. They told her what to say on television. They put her on the cover of their magazines. They told
all of their readers and followers to read her. They analyzed
the motives behind the male reviewers' unfavorable reviews
before they'd even appeared. They arranged her trips and
tours; they called up the hotels; they bought her tickets; they
would have flown the planes if asked; they got her on "The
Today Show," "CBS Morning News," network night shows,
call-in shows, and kept her on Broadway for six months breaking all records, and here she was calling white women all
kinds of bitches and telling him what he should do for the
sisters. He thought about the picture of her on the podium at
Town Hall, kissing some elderly southern novelist; almost
knocking her over with affection, and how she said, when she
won her honor, that she wanted to spend the time with Becky
and celebrate her success with all of her friends.

Up north, Ball decided, things were awfully complex. He
couldn't wait until the day after the opening of his play. He
would go south, visit his mother for a few weeks.

15

He'd received a call from Becky French that morning. Can
you please get over here this morning at 9:30 A.M. No hello or
nothing. When he reached the office, Mr. Ickey, the receptionist, the man with Humpty Dumpty's shape, lacking any

perceptible waist, peered up at him. He smiled a decadent sleazy smile. Probably a frustrated romantic, Ball thought. Ickey signaled for him to go in and returned to reading the newspaper. Ball could hear the discussion coming from behind the door. He recognized Tremonisha's voice.

"You're going to change the entire meaning of the play. You hell hussy. Everything you touch you corrupt." The voice that replied was equally shrill.

"I'm not going to produce that play as it is. We have . . . standards to uphold." In his mind's eye, he could see Becky shake her head like a filly when she said *standards*.

"It's not standards. You're worried about that monologue. It's political, isn't it? You don't like the monologue, you bitch, admit it. You white feminists sound more like the white man with each passing day. In fact, the only thing your dipshit movement has produced is more white men. Standards. All the mediocre shit that you produce by these junior womanists. You've got your nerve talking about standards. Why do you always feel the need to castrate the black man?"

"How can you say that? You're the one they picketed." That remark from French was followed by silence.

"That was your fault. You and that mutant bacteria out there. Your assistant. You were the one who listed me as a spokesperson for all black women in that press release. Writing The Black Woman's story. You insisted that I write in the scene about the man throwing his wife, the missionary, downstairs. In my version, she only converts him. You wanted to sensationalize it."

"I don't remember."

"All of you white bitches are like that. You don't remember. You treacherous cunt. Every time I'd appear on television you'd call. Telling me how I didn't sound like a dedicated feminist. How I should change my hairdo. How I ought to put more punch into my attack on black men. What's you bitches' hang-up about black men anyway? You're more likely to be raped by your daddy, your brother, or your date, man or woman."

"Tremonisha, have you been taking Valium again? I told you about that. It makes you sound, well, you know, unreasonable."

"It's not the Valium, it's you, you're the biggest depressant I know."

"Look, Ms., I made you and I can destroy you. I filled that theater with women and got you those interviews in the magazines. You were nothing. Reading your diatribes in quaint little coffee shops on the Lower East Side. I created you. I gave you prominence. But don't get smart. There's always somebody else who'll take your place."

"Do me like you did Johnnie Kranshaw, huh? Whatever became of her? Where did she go? Answer me, bitch, where did she go!"

Ball used the silence that followed as an opportunity to enter the office. He cleared his throat. They were both frozen toward each other like two cats with humped backs. Their jaws were puffed. He could smell the violence. Becky was lighting a cigarette, her hands trembling, and Tremonisha was staring at her, her hands on her hips.

"You're not to come into this office unless you knock," Becky said. She was shaking like a wet dog.

"I'm sorry, the receptionist told me to come in."

"You don't have to apologize, Ian. This bitch wants to fuck with your play. The same way they did with mine."

"Look, Tre, nobody was twisting your arm," Becky said, cuttingly. They were staring at each other. Their chests were heaving. "Nobody begged you, Tre. You didn't complain as long as the money was coming in. As long as you could take those trips to Europe, to learn and to grow, as you put it. You didn't complain then." Tremonisha looked at the floor.

"I was young."

"Maybe you want to be alone. I can leave," Ball said.

"Tell him what you want to do with his play. She wants to change your play so that the mob victim is just as guilty as the mob. She wants to drop Cora Mae's line about their being in the same boat. That's that collective guilt bullshit that's part of this jive New York intellectual scene. She wants you to change the whole meaning of the play. She's saying that the man who reckless eyeballed Cora Mae was just as guilty as the men who murdered him. She feels that Ham Hill's staring at Cora was tantamount to a violent act. If looks could kill? Huh, Becky? She's saying that Ham Hill murdered Cora with his eyes." Tremonisha and Becky were exchanging stares that were so dense he felt that they were probably looking right through each other.

He thought of them in the same households all over the Americas while the men were away on long trips to the international centers of the cotton or sugar markets. The secrets they exchanged in the night when there were no men around, during the Civil War in America when the men were in the battlefield and the women were in the house. Black and white, sisters and half-sisters. Mistresses and wives. There was something going on here that made him, a man, an outsider, a spectator, like someone who'd stumbled into a country where people talked in sign language and he didn't know the signs. After a long silence Becky said, turning to him: "I just want you to tone it down a little."

As a climax to this extraordinary scene, Tremonisha started for the door. "Come on, Ian. Buy me a drink. Let's get out of here. First she cuts the white women out of the lynching scene, and next she wants you to change the whole meaning of the play." Ball stood there. He thought of a long article he'd read about how plays about women were hot, and that anybody who could put together a halfway decent one could be assured of a performance. And anyway, what did this argument between these women have to do with him? Hadn't the black ones said that the only thing that had happened since Martin Luther King, Jr., was the black woman, and weren't the white ones telling themselves that they had come a long way baby? What did a quarrel between these sisters, hugging each other one minute and scratching out each other's eyes the next have to do with him? "Well, Ball," Tre finally said. "Are you coming?" He stood his ground. She went to the door and slammed it, but not before giving them both disgusted looks. Ian turned to Becky and said: "Can we talk?" She smiled.

Paul Shoboater, critic for the *Downtown Mandarin*, kept Ian waiting. He looked at his watch. Paul was forty-five minutes late. He was like that, especially toward up-north fellas. They were from the same neck of the woods, but back home he and Paul didn't move in the same circles. Shoboater had been in the North as long as Ball had, but refused to drop his down home accent. Shoboater knew that Ball would probably be uncomfortable in this kind of place, with its white and black checkerboard tile floor, and waitresses in black silk dresses and white aprons, and tuxedoed waiters. Ball sat at the bar, sipping from a glass of Pabst Blue Ribbon.

The bartender had sighed when Ball ordered it. Shoboater finally entered, or swept in. He saw Ball, but pretended not to notice him as he greeted some of his friends. Artists and critics from the downtown art scene. He finally reached the spot where Ball was seated, and gave him a cool handshake. The maitre d' came up bowing and scraping before Shoboater, greeting him as he escorted the pair to Shoboater's reserved table. Ball followed Shoboater, carrying his Pabst with him and finally placing it on the white linen tablecloth. When the waiter asked them what kind of cocktails they wanted, Shoboater ordered some vintage wine, and Ball ordered another Pabst. The waiter and Shoboater shared a chuckle. The fellas called Shoboater "Eye Spy" because they claimed that his column for the *Mandarin* was actually a literary reconnaissance mission for tourists who wanted to become acquaintances with the trends and styles of Afro-American culture. An expedition into the heart of darkness, as it were. The fellas claimed that his position made him lazy because his editors didn't know whether he was faking it or telling the truth. Others said that his real role was that of a hit man for modernism, Pound's "botched bitch gone in the teeth" reeling from blow after successive blow. The modernists could take Sartre's late disavowal of existentialism, and the failure of Marxism, or even the death of abstract expressionism, but Freud's fall, that was the severest blow, and finished off the movement that had been traveling a steady intellectual downhill since the revelations about Stalinism. Freud had achieved the status of a Holy Man for them.

Brashford had claimed that the Jews ran the *Downtown Mandarin*, and that even though it carried articles that opposed quotas and affirmative action as methods for subsidizing blacks, fifty percent of the revenue of Jewish organizations was derived from government subsidies, and though they had put Shoboater up to claiming that black talent got by because of liberal guilt, the same thing was said about Jewish talent in the fifties; that the rise of the American Jewish novelist coincided with a wave of guilt that swept the country after the discovery of the Holocaust. The fellas also ridiculed Shoboater's "showout" ornamental prose style that made his work nearly unreadable—they said that if his prose style were a horse someone would have put it out of its misery long ago.

After a weak toast to Ball's play, Shoboater skimmed through Ball's script as though Ball wasn't even sitting there. Ball could tell that this was the first occasion upon which Shoboater had availed himself of reading the manuscript. When the waiter came up and asked for their orders, Shoboater ordered in impeccable French, which must have impressed the waiter because he had a huge smile while scribbling the order. They both looked at Ball, who said that he would have the same thing as Shoboater.

"So what is this crazy shit of yours that the Lord Mountbatten is doing?" Shoboater said.

"It's not going to be done at the Mountbatten. They've moved it over to the Queen Mother," Ball said, choking on his pride. Shoboater grinned widely when he heard that.

"*Reckless Eyeballing*, heh. Nigger, you are crazy, like they say." Ball wanted to knock his teeth out right there. But thought better of it. He gritted his teeth and in his mind's eye saw Paul Shoboater falling from the chair and cracking his skull against one of those stone pillars of the restaurant, or the heavy pot that held ferns. He saw the waiter rise from where Paul lay—blood pouring from his head, spattering his three-piece French-cut suit—shaking his head before the shocked fellow diners, and announcing, "He's dead."

"And Ham Hill. Why Ham Hill?"

"Ham Hill gets lynched for staring at this southern white woman. I call him that because it's kind of like Ham in the Bible, who gets cursed to be "black" and "elongated" for staring at Noah's nakedness. Brashford tells me, however, that this version was perpetuated by a Jewish commentator and can't be found in the Bible."

"Well, I hope you don't think that's anything original," Shoboater said sarcastically. "All over the world there are legends and myths about men staring at women or staring into their eyes or at them bathing, and being cursed."

"I didn't say anything about it being new," Ball said. Their lunch arrived. It looked like vomit. Some kind of veal covered with a rich, creamy sauce. Shoboater began to eat; Ball pushed his plate away and continued to drink from his second Pabst. He couldn't understand why Paul sneered at Pabst. If you ever examined the can or bottle closely you could see the reproduction of the medals the beer had received in international competitions with other beers, he thought. Shoboater kept scribbling in a leather-bound notebook with a red fountain pen that probably cost about five hundred dollars.

"Why are you so hung up on eyes? I remember in that travesty of yours, *Suzanna*, there were a lot of eye monologues and dialogues."

"Eyes reveal a person's true intentions. They are, as Rousseau said, the soul's mirror. I also like to provide my actors and actresses an opportunity to do mime. I use the term 'reckless eyeballing' because on one level the play is about people intruding into spaces that don't concern them."

"Yeah. Well, you might try to rationalize it that way, but it seems to me that you're trying to make amends for your awful reputation as a male chauvinist. Admit it. The tables have turned since the seventies and now this women's thing is hot, you're trying to cash in on it."

"That's your opinion, Paul."

"My opinion, huh. Clever of you, I must admit. That bit about this woman having the body of Ham Hill exhumed twenty years after his lynching in hopes that a new trial might erase the lingering doubts that she brought the attention of his eyes upon herself—that is hilarious. Just like those dizzy feminists. I like that." He chuckled, but in his column he was always pretending to be a feminist or a womanist, probably because women wielded some power at the *Mandarin*. There was something odd and weird about Paul. Come to think of it, the nigger did resemble Peter Lorre a bit with his Dr. Moto spectacles, his whiney, nasal voice.

"I'm glad you liked that," Ball said, watching him eat the

veal and sauce. Just watching him eat it made him feel nauseous.

Ball looked around because he felt some heat at the back of his neck. A woman dressed in the art nouveau fashion of the restaurant was staring at him, but when he caught her eyes, she fluttered them nervously and stared again toward her male companion. Lot's wife, Ball thought.

"What do you think happened to Minsk?" Shoboater asked.

"I don't know."

"So they got Tremonisha to direct."

"Yeah," Ball said, looking down at his beer. He grinned.

"But you were the one who went about bad-mouthing her after *Wrong-Headed Man* hit the big time. What made you change?" He grinned even wider.

"I've matured. You know my play *Suzanna*, well, it was written at a time when these guys were into a big macho thing. You know, going around bragging about how they knocked this bitch over and that bitch over. Now we've entered a new period. I've grown with the times. I'm used to working with Jim, but I can adjust, I am adjusting."

"Yeah. The Jews were the only ones keeping you guys going. But instead of expressing gratitude, the fellas keep coming down hard on the Jews, and commenting on the Middle East when most of you don't even know where it is on the map. Instead of fighting the Jews, you ought to be like them. They've survived all of their enemies, the Assyrians, the Babylonians, the Persians, the Pharonic and Ptolemaic Egyptians, Rome. All dead. In fifty years they will have outlived the Germans, a vanishing race hung up on Föhn. Germany's population growth is zero. They don't have the will to continue. It's as though they've been obeahed or dybukked. Günter Grass has written a book about it: *Headbirths, or The Germans Are Dying Out*." He kept on yammering about how the blacks ought to be like Jews. The waiter took the plates away. Ball was glad. He was really getting sick. How could Shoboater eat that shit, he thought.

"These blacks ought to save their money instead of loafing around and break-dancing."

"Brashford said that the reason the Jews came up with monotheism is because they were too cheap to buy idols."

"You're still hanging out with him, huh. He hasn't written a play in over twenty years and the only reason they're still backing him is because of that long monologue in the middle of his one and only play where the character renounces militancy and the end where that black guy comes out dressed in drag. He knew what he was doing. And then in the epilogue all of the black male bar patrons go off and register for World War Two so's they could fight Hitler. That's how the clever second-rate writer got to Broadway. That monologue in the middle and the ending. That's what got him over. The producers propped him up so that they wouldn't have to deal with Randy Shank. Incidentally, what happened to him? He was quite a character."

"He's working uptown as a doorman at Tremonisha's apartment building." Shoboater got a big kick out of that. He thought it to be so hilarious that he didn't stop cackling for a couple of minutes.

"Serves him right. He alienated the women, the Jews, and now he's out on the street. All those things he said about the Jews. Now he's suffering the retribution that eventually catches up with all of their enemies. That Jehovah, or Jah, is the Dirty Harry among the gods. He don't play. You fuck with his people, he'll get you. Now you know if he punishes his own followers so harshly, calling the children of Israel harlots and nasty things for disobeying him, you can imagine what he has in store for his people's enemies. The Jews are the only ones standing between black people and these barbarians from Europe that are over here. What do you think that the Posse Comitatus, the Order, and the other right-wing outpatient clinic is talking about when they say "bleeding heart liberals." They're talking about the Jews. Plain and simple. And every year I send one-tenth of my salary to the Anti-Defamation

League because they're keeping an eye on these people who not only hate the Jews but hate blacks too. You can't depend upon this black middle-class to do that, or the black intellectuals. All of them have become buppies. They spend an hour sometimes talking about condos and these wine-tasting clubs they belong to, or their computers. If it wasn't for Jewish morality these people would be burning niggers left and right. The Jews went into Europe and civilized these Anglos Nordics and Germans who were painting themselves blue and eating one another. Go read their texts. Read *Hamlet*—the play that tells you about the Nordic soul: a cold-blooded serial murderer who kills all of these people because he heard voices. Man, the only difference between Son of Sam and Hamlet is that Hamlet speaks blank verse. And their music, full of killing, like those Wagnerian operas where people ride into fire and things. Man, that's where this whole idea of nuclear war comes from. When one travels through Europe and visits the museums as I have done"—big deal, Ball thought—"one is struck by the violence on those walls. If violence is as American as apple pie, then Europe provided the oven, because on the public buildings, in the churches, and in the paintings there are scenes of violence. People stabbing one another and hacking each other to pieces, or beheading one another, and when there are no scenes of that they're killing dragons. Armies clashing and people wrapped up by snakes. They even have these women warriors there, Amazons who are dealing blows to men left and right. It's all over the place. The most frequent object you see in European art is a weapon. And their stories. Full of murder and mayhem. Man, if the Jews hadn't gone in there and tried to civilize these people with their blood-thirsty Viking gods, these people would still be on the rampage. And every time there's a period of reaction against compassion and mercy, these gods start to rumble again. They even named this new laser weapon The Excalibur; they can't get swords out of their minds. If Judaism hadn't required those people to renounce their blood-thirsty war gods, the world would have been finished long ago." The waiter brought Shoboater a tiny cup full of espresso. Ball was on his third Pabst.

"Man, is that all you're going to drink? You don't touch your food. I'm on an expense account. What's the matter with you?"

"I'm not hungry," Ball said.

"Black people are strongest when they emulate the Jews. How do you think they got through slavery? Those old biblical metaphors, that's how. They used them. They identified with the children of Israel. That's how they survived their suffering. Through the gospel they were able to define their situation. These intellectuals who denounce the Jews are making the same mistake that Hitler made."

"I don't understand."

"If Hitler had listened to the Jews, he would have won the war."

"How's that?"

"The V-1 rocket designed at Peenemünde was the ancestor of the modern missile. It would have enabled Hitler to strike England and the U.S. with A-bombs. He rejected the A-bomb. Called the theory behind it 'Jewish physics.' His wrong-headed bigotry finally did him in."

"Tremonisha says that Hitler was Jewish and that the reason he hated the Jews was because he actually hated himself, or wanted the approval of white people."

"She got it all wrong. It was the German nation that tried to become white. You ask a Swede, a Norwegian or a Dane, or an Icelander whether the Germans are Nordic, as Hitler claimed, and he will laugh in your face. I mean, this Nibelungen thing that Hitler was raving about—it doesn't even belong to the Germans. It's under lock and key in a museum in Reykjavik. It's the sacred work of the Nordic people. Written on cowhide, and in different colors of ink. The Ger-

mans have too much Tartar blood to be Nordic. The Khans
left onion-shaped domes all over Germany, and that is not all
they left. Hitler probably had more Mongol blood than anything else; most of those people come out of central Asia.
There's still no hard evidence that Hitler was Jewish, regardless
of what Tremonisha says. It was the German nation that went
crazy trying to be white; they tried everything, they tried to
claim the Greeks, they tried to claim the Egyptians. Nothing
worked, and so Hitler came along and said *you're white* so
often that they believed it, and so for as long as Hitler was in
power, every German person stood in front of his mirror and
didn't see himself, but saw a blond, blue-eyed Aryan. Talking
about schizophrenia. He had them mesmerized.

"As for Tre, they don't even understand her plays. But as
long as she takes swipes at the brothers, Becky will keep her."
He leaned over. Whispering. "Between you and me, I think
it's because of some affair Becky had when she was in the
South organizing during the sixties. Some black dude. Fucked
over her. Stole her credit cards, and forged her checks, and
now she's using Tremonisha to get even with all black men.
Kind of like a circus act where the ringmaster shoots a dummy
out of a cannon. She dared not tamper with your play because
of Jim Minsk. I'm surprised that they even gave you a workshop, now that he's dead."

"Brashford says that the Jews are using blacks to keep the
goyim off their case. All this stuff about pathology—welfare,
crime and dope, single parent households—he says that the
conservative Jews keep those issues on the front burner so's the
goyim will be so angry with blacks that they will ignore the Jews
and leave them alone. He says that the black criminals might
mug somebody or relieve them of a gold chain, but they never
built no empire of crime like Murder Incorporated like the
Jews did."

"Ninety-five percent of the audience for his stuff is Jewish.
The blacks don't like him, nor his work. Listen, you're going

to have to wean yourself away from Brashford. Hasn't he gotten you enough grants and fellowships? I mean, it must be embarrassing."

Ball didn't say anything. The waiter came and handed Shoboater the check. He pulled out his American Express and signed for it.

"I got to hand it to you, Ball. You're the original malevolent rabbit. You couldn't care less about what happened to Brashford. As soon as you stop using him, you'll use somebody else. Your mother was like that. Wasn't she arrested?" Ball leaned over and grabbed the sucker by the collar. The diners looked at the pair, but Ball didn't care. He let him go. Shoboater was trembling.

"Hey man. Calm down. Here, have some coffeè, it's like the kind they have down home. None of this weak northern stuff." He poured Ball some coffee from the silver pot the waiter had left.

"I'm sorry, Paul. But when somebody puts my mother down, I just go crazy." Besides, he wanted Shoboater to write a good review of *Reckless Eyeballing*.

"So Randy Shank is a doorman uptown," Shoboater said, changing the subject, smiling profusely and straightening his clothes.

"He's an important playwright. He paved the way for us all. Now that he's down on his luck, you guys are pouncing on him like buzzards, lingering over his bones."

Shoboater looked at his watch. "Hey, I'm late. I have to go uptown for the interview with—" He mentioned the name of another black feminist writer who had finished a book.

She wrote in a style that Brashford sarcastically called "finishing school lumpen." Brashford accused the woman of having maimed the speech of ghetto women for the benefit of white women who didn't know any better.

He rose and hurried out of the restaurant. The tailor-made suit had his butt sticking out. That amused Ball.

"Anything else, monsieur?" the waiter asked.

"Yeah. Give me another Pabst," Ball said. The waiter turned up his nose.

That night he dreamed that all of those giant Amazon women that Shoboater had said were on the walls of museums on the domed ceilings of churches, and on public buildings in Europe had escaped and were chasing him and the fellas through the streets. These giant women didn't seem to have much difficulty in catching them, despite the heavy clothing they were wearing. None of them tripped over her skirt. They were "monstropolous," as Zora Neale Hurston would say.

O'Reedy was getting nowhere with his search for the Flower Phantom. The bastard's somewhere right now, probably laughing at me, he thought as he entered his house in Queens. He hung up his coat and hat in the hall.

"Where's dinner?" he said gruffly. He heard low voices talking in the living room. He couldn't make out what they were saying.

He sees things. I think that he needs a rest, and the other day he didn't know that I was in the house, and he was in the bedroom with that thing.

What thing?

That gun. He had it next to him.

Maybe he was keeping it under the pillow.

No, he had it next to his cheek. He had a smile on his face.
I'll try to talk Dad into taking a vacation.
He calls the gun Nancy. I mean, Sean, I wouldn't . . . I
mean I've been a good wife, and, well, if it was another
woman, I'd understand, and even another man, I mean, I try
to keep up with the times, but Sean, competing with a gun—
He stood in the doorway. He cleared his throat.

"Oh, dear, we didn't hear you come in, Sean is here."

"Yeah, I see him with my own eyes. So what were you two
gabbing about?" He folded his arms and leaned against one
side of the threshold.

"We, ah, we—" his wife began. "Oh, I'd better see about
dinner." She went into the kitchen, leaving Sean to his father.
His son looked more like O'Reedy's father, Captain Timothy
O'Reedy, who was known as a great risk taker, and finally
made captain after a controversial career and many unneces-
sary homicides, which he claimed took place in the line of
duty. Freckled face, red hair, but unlike his grandfather Sean
O'Reedy was a wimp, in the eyes of his dad. He was thirty-five
years old and still in school.

"Mom and I were thinking, Dad, you've built all of this
vacation time up, maybe you ought to take a vacation, kind of
get your schedule ready for retirement."

"I haven't missed a day's work in the thirty years I've been
on the force." O'Reedy picked up the newspaper from the
doorway entrance and sat down on a sofa and began reading as
though Sean wasn't even there. On the wall of the living room
were framed portraits of the Virgin Mary, Queen Elizabeth
and Prince Philip. The queen was seated. The wall also bore a
painting of a landscape, and there were furnishings that elitists
would consider kitsch. He could smell the roast beef coming
from the kitchen.

"Staying for dinner?" O'Reedy asked, not even taking time
to look up from his paper. The headlines read: FLOWER PHAN-
TOM STRIKES AGAIN.

"I don't think so, Dad, I have a date tonight."

"Yeah, when do you think you're going to settle down? Your mother keeps talking about grandchildren." O'Reedy was uncomfortable being left in the same room with Sean. Something about the kid was strange. Always into the books, never any time for fun, and when O'Reedy took him to some chippies to get him broken in, the kid ran away. Scared of broads.

"Dad, I came to say goodbye." O'Reedy looked up.

"Goodbye, what do you mean, goodbye?"

"I'm going to California, Dad. I'm going to be teaching Irish studies." His father slowly lowered the newspaper from his face.

"Irish what?"

"Irish studies. I've been hired by a foundation that's begun an institute in ethnic studies."

"And what was it again that you were going to teach?"

"Irish studies."

"And what, may I ask, is that?"

"It's the study of Irish culture, history, politics, literature—" O'Reedy laughed as his lanky son stood before him dressed in a tweed jacket, green turtleneck sweater, jeans, and sneakers.

"Hey, you come here." His wife came into the room, but not before turning down the portable television's volume. Bette Davis was giving Anne Baxter a good scolding on the subject of ambition.

"Tell her what you told me."

"He's teaching Irish studies, he told me all about it," she said.

"Both of you are nuts," O'Reedy said, rising. "I thought that you'd finally come to your senses. Thought that you might go into something worthwhile. The high tech stuff. Now that's where the money is. I said give him time. He'll shape up. Settle down. But no, none of these neighborhood girls are good enough for you. Downtown freaks, like that . . . the one you brought into your mother's house, didn't like me using the word broad or chick. And now this Irish studies. All about stupid micks."

"Dad, don't say that."

"I think he's doing the right thing, dear," Mrs. O'Reedy said.

"Who's asking you. Get back into the kitchen."

"Yes, dear," she said, returning to the kitchen.

"What can you learn about Irishmen in a university that you can't learn down at the local gin mill?"

"Look, I have to go, Dad. My date."

"Probably some fucking hippie like the last one. Kept interrupting all of the male guests with her crazy ideas, embarrassing me in front of my buddies and their wives. She wouldn't even offer to help with the dishes. Yet you got all high and mighty when I tried to introduce you to those hookers that time when I was trying to help you learn things."

"You hate yourself, Pop, you're Irish, yet you don't think that the Irish have produced anything worthwhile. You and your father, just carrying out the orders of people who hate you, who treat you no differently than they would a stage Irishman, a clown—"

"Now, you wait—" O'Reedy said, rising.

"A great Irish-American writer like James T. Farrell had to borrow money from friends because the Irish were so busy trying to assimilate that they didn't support their artistic geniuses, ignored them because they were considered too ethnic by people on the make. Reminded them of a world they wanted to leave behind, and so they use your pop—"

"How would you like to get a good belt—"

"That's right. Be their Dirty Harry Callahan. If you can't get your way, use violence. You're like the middle men all over the world, the muscle, the fists for people who spit on your kind, you're protecting their property by beating up people. You and your father, both mercenaries. At the turn of the century they used your father against the Jews on the Lower

East Side and against other Irish. Why do you think they call those vehicles that transport prisoners paddy wagons? Did you ever think of that? And now they use you against the blacks and the Puerto Ricans."

"That's enough outta you."

"Don't think I don't know about those three Spanish guys and that jogger—" O'Reedy knocked his son over the sofa he was standing in front of.

"Get up! Get up! I'll teach you." His wife ran from the kitchen screaming.

"You keep out of this," he said. One Spanish guy was standing behind Sean. He was thumb-nosing O'Reedy, mocking him. The other two Spanish guys sat on the edge of the couch behind which Sean was beginning to rise. One had a radio next to his head and the other was popping his fingers. They were wearing party shirts and dark glasses. O'Reedy stepped back, a look of horror on his face.

"Dad, what's wrong?" Sean said. As he said that, the black jogger ran through the room, entering through one wall and exiting through another. O'Reedy went for his gun, but before he could fire Sean knocked it out of his hand.

"I . . ." his father was in a daze. Sean and Mrs. O'Reedy escorted him to the couch.

"I'll be all right. I just need a drink. Son, I'm sorry, I just haven't . . ."

"It's all right," Sean said, going to the kitchen to remove a bottle of whiskey from the cabinet. O'Reedy's wife remained in the room. She sat next to him on the couch. He put his head in her lap and began to sob.

"Don't worry, dear," she said. "You'll be retiring soon."

18

Opening night. The play was going splendidly. The ninety-nine people were sitting on top of one another, and must have been uncomfortable, but they were paying close attention to the developments onstage. Tremonisha had supervised every detail: costumes, lighting, props, sets, et cetera. But where was Tre? He'd called her house, but there hadn't been an answer for a week or so. Nobody had seen her since their encounter in the office where her blowup with Becky had taken place. Becky had brought in another director who merely supervised the details of mounting the play that Tre had created. Becky insisted that Tre's version of the play not be tampered with. They waited a half hour after the scheduled opening time for her to show up, but when she didn't they decided to begin. She'd worked out every detail with such professionalism that there was really no need for her now. Ian's respect for her had certainly increased, and he hoped that she'd never learn what he and the fellas said about her behind her back, all of the scurrilous, unprintable things. They talked about Clotel the mulatto and Coretha the black woman, and how they and their Native-American, Asian, and Hispanic sisters had had babies by every conceivable European man from the tip of Argentina to the Arctic—how they'd performed the hemispheric sixty-nine with Frenchmen, Dutchmen, Spaniards, Portuguese, Russians, British, Scots, Irishmen, and God knows what other kind of European white eyes.

Act I was a tremendous hit, with some of the audience breaking into applause after particularly dramatic lines and speeches. The only male member of the cast was the skeleton of Ham Hill, which they'd borrowed from one of the local medical schools. The play opened with the female judge, who wore her hair in a dignified bun, Cora Mae, her lawyer, Ham Hill's lawyer, played by an excellent black actress, though on the plump side—but the casting director had said that they'd lose one-third of the white male audience if they didn't include "a ham," as this type of actress was called—the female jury, and female bailiff. Even the two gravediggers were female. They all stood around the grave as the coffin of Ham Hill was raised. Ball had included some telling eye exchanges in this scene. Ham Hill's defense lawyer, who was wearing a black pin-striped suit, white silk blouse, and huge black bow tie, her hair straightened and glossy, was glaring with contempt at the plaintiff, Cora Mae, now a radical feminist lesbian, part owner of a bookstore, and her lover, a woman with short hair, a round face, and wearing glasses. The two embraced and sobbed as the coffin lid was raised. Cora Mae's lawyer, who was dressed like one of the female executives one sees in Ms. magazine—attaché case, business suit—remained expressionless during the entire scene, which ended with the skeleton of Ham Hill being removed from the coffin and placed into a patrol car—offstage—for the trip to the courthouse, accompanied by thunder, lightning, and great applause. Though one drunken black male first-nighter was ejected from the theater for standing and shouting—"Looks like a case of dig the nigger up and kill him again."

The second act took place inside the courtroom and was highlighted by Ham Hill's attorney demolishing the testimony of Cora Mae. She showed the jury photos of Cora as she appeared twenty years before, in the sixties, with heavy makeup, miniskirt, eye shadow, rouge, blond hair with black roots: a sleaze and a tease. Over the objection of Cora's defense lawyer, Ham Hill's attorney said that there was no difference between Cora Mae and the man who opens his coat and displays his genitals to females in public places. Her description of Cora Mae as a flasher brought an eruption of discussion from the courtroom, whereupon the judge banged the gavel for order. Cora Mae, the defense attorney claimed, craved attention from men and only complained about Ham Hill when she noticed that Ham Hill wasn't staring at her in the fateful encounter outside the supermarket where Ham Hill worked as a packer. At that moment the skeleton, with a sardonic grin, began to slide to the floor; the bailiff propped it up. This gesture by the corpse, as if done to make a point, was applauded wildly by the audience. The judge overruled the objections of Cora Mae's lawyer, stating that Ms. Mae's reputation in the sixties was certainly relevant to the case. The second act ended with Cora Mae's lover—both of them were dressed in men's clothes and looked as though they'd just climbed from beneath a manhole—jumping to her feet and complaining about Cora's treatment and the judge citing the woman for contempt and ejecting her from the courtroom. It took five strong women to accomplish this deed.

During the intermission Ball went out into the lobby. Average everyday normal middle-class people were congratulating him and patting him on the back, while the white feminists stared at him stonily. He could tell that their black feminist friends had really enjoyed the performance of Ham Hill's defense attorney but wouldn't let on before their white sisters; one came up to him later and told him so. The fellas had said that a lot of feminists were okay when you had a one-on-one relationship with them, but when they were around the sisters they'd get all fired up. The academic black Marxist-Leninists were in one corner sneering, and the black avant-garde members of the audience segregated themselves from the rest of the people in the lobby. They were standing near the wall, sulking.

Drat them, Ball thought. He figured that he had it made. The third act would begin with Cora Mae back on the stand. Under questioning, Cora Mae would reveal that it took her twenty years to bring charges against Ham Hill, the lynch mob victim, because she'd been converted from a rock and roll sex kitten to a radical feminist and was only now capable of assessing the heinousness of Ham Hill's crime. That she felt it was important to clear her name. That if there was no trial, there'd always be the suspicion that she was trying to lure Ham Hill, the supermarket packer, who'd been lynched by her husband and his friends. That sex with her husband was no good after the incident and that he'd spent many nights during their married life pacing the floor and sitting on the porch, staring at the stars. She would testify that her social life had been ruined until she took up with her lover and opened the radical lesbian bookstore. The audience would hiss and catcall at this explanation, Ball was sure. Confident, Ball decided to leave the workshop performance of his play and head upstairs to the Lord Mountbatten, where "the important play" was taking place. As he walked up the aisle well-wishers touched his elbows or shook his hands.

They had the Lord Mountbatten set up like a German cabaret of the 1930s. The audience was seated at tables, and was being served liquor and sandwiches. The actress playing Eva Braun sat on a dressing room bench before a large mirror. It was supposed to be her bedroom inside the Führerbunker. She was adjusting a bridal headdress and powdering her face. She wore a frilly pink slip and was speaking her lines to the audience through the mirror. A tiny orchestra of tuba, trombone, two violins, saxophone, bass, and drums was positioned behind the mirror. On one flat board that represented the bedroom's wall was a photo of Klara Hitler, Hitler's mother, who looked like the dictator. Ms. Braun must have just made some kind of pungent point because as Ball entered, the audience of mostly women was applauding loudly. He sat down at one of the ta- bles and the two women who were occupying the other chairs frowned. During the scene the sound person had simulated the noise of airplanes and bombing taking place in the background.

"Now he's going to marry me. Now that the enemy is closing in, he wants to tie the knot. Well, I have news for him." (The audience applauds wildly and Becky French, seated with her party of feminist celebrities at the front table, beams out over the audience. She notices Ball. Ball waves at her, but she ignores him.) "All these nights he kept me locked up in this Romanesque cemetery with its stone walls and security guards while he was gallivanting all over Europe. I knew what he was doing. Don't think that I'm not aware of the other women. All of them, Goebbels, Göring with his big bovine bitch of a wife, and his cream-colored uniforms. Don't think that little Eva doesn't know what's going on."

(Audience applauds madly.)

"As for Der Führer, as he calls himself, he nearly screwed his little niece Geli to death because he couldn't deal with an older, more mature woman. They said that Geli committed suicide, but I know. He killed her because she got pregnant by a Jew. A woman that would come between him and Klara, his mother. Look at that bitch." (She points to the photo of Klara Hitler hanging on the wall.) "Boy, was she a nudge." She walks up and down the floor with her hands on her hips, occasionally making sweeping gestures with one hand. She's constantly smoking a cigarette. "'Adolf, why do you want to go to Vienna to study art? Adolf, why don't you try to settle into a legitimate business?''Yes, mama.' Boy, was he devoted to her. Even spared the Jewish doctor who took care of her. As for his thing about the Jews—well, everybody knows why he does that. They talk about him behind his back. Those insane speeches he makes when he's had all of that cocaine and heroin. The Jewish problem. The only Jewish problem Germany has is him." (Applause.) "God, that woman has been dead these many years, but she still controls him. Sometimes when he's making love to me, if you want to call it that, he calls out her name. Klara. Oh, Klara. It's disgusting. And if you knew what I know about him in bed, then you'd understand why he's trying to conquer all of these countries and be such a big man." (The actor playing Hitler emerges from where he's been seated in the audience and joins Eva, the spotlight following him. There's a chorus of boos from the women in the audience. The trombone makes a clownish sound, and there's a clash of cymbals from the drummer.) "Eva. Eva. The allies are bickering among themselves, according to the shortwave. There's hope yet. Are you ready? The preacher will be here soon." (He rushes back into the audience, the spotlight following him. Eva turns to the audience.) "That's that cocaine and heroin talking. There's no way he's going to get out of this place alive. That's his problem," she says, lighting a cigarette. (A black woman in the audience says, "Tell it, honey." Other women join in. "Tell it, honey," followed by titters. The two women at Ball's table smile at him. He turns his eyes away.) "Well, I'm not going to be like those other women." (Wild applause.) "Eva's got some sense." (More applause. Hitler emerges from the audience again, this time with a priest in priestly garb carrying a Bible.)

"Eva. Are you ready, my sweet?"(Eva, to audience: "Watch this.")

"Ready for what?" (She turns toward the two men. The priest gets a load of her thighs where the slip line ends. She crosses her legs. His eyes grow large and he almost drops his Bible.)

"Ready for the wedding, Eva. Eva. You're not even dressed." (Eva rises.)

"Look, you little shrimp. I'm not going to stand for this dreckscheisse any longer." (Both the priest and the Führer are horrified. The audience laughs and applauds.)

"Eva, what's come over you? Father, she doesn't know what she's saying."

"I do know what I'm saying. Boy, did you have me fooled. All that sweet talk about destiny and how you were going to get me a job as a Hollywood film editor. I should have known."

"Eva, what are you talking about?" Hitler says.

"While you were away getting yours I was here getting mine, or as the American song says, you should have been concerned about who was making love to your old lady while you were out making love." (This line brings the house down.)

"Eva, you've been listening to those nigger records. I'm going to take them away from you." (A huge, blond, blue-eyed chauffeur approaches the front from the audience. Eva turns to him.)

"Are you ready, Otto?" (Otto nods.)

Hitler says, "Eva, what is the meaning of this?" (Stunned, Hitler turns to the priest, who shrugs his shoulders.) "I'm going to get married all right, but not to you. I'm marrying Otto," Eva says, closing her eyes and bobbing her leg in defiance. (The priest sneaks a glance at her legs.)

"You and him!!" To Otto: "Otto, you're a loyal German, I need you."

"He's not German, he's Jewish." (The audience goes wild.) "A better man than you will ever be." The priest says, "But he has blue eyes, and an Aryan nose."

"Many Jews have such features," Eva says. "Besides, I decided, why should I have a half-breed when I can have the real thing." (Eva removes a revolver from the dressing table drawer. Hitler and the priest do a double take and take a few steps backward.) "My own private, intimate gun, where—what are you doing?" Hitler says.

"I went through your coat pocket. That's where I found the names and telephone numbers of Christian women you've been screwing all over Europe. Now you two get on your knees. Get their guns, Otto." (Delighted, the audience applauds. Otto goes over and takes Hitler's gun.)

"Please don't shoot. Why, I'm the savior of the German nation, the German nation is like . . . well . . . a bride to me."

"And so you treated her like your other women. Destroyed her because she couldn't measure up to your mother." (Otto grins.) She fires shots into Hitler, after each one reciting a specific crime. "This is for tortured France. This is for ravished Poland. This is for maimed Czechoslovakia. This is for Mother Russia. This is for all of the women you've ruined . . . my sisters." (The audience is on its feet applauding, hooting, cheering, and the two women sharing a table with Ball stare at Ball, menacingly. Come to think of it, he's the only man in attendance.)

"Please don't shoot me," the priest says. "It was his fault. He made me do it. He made all of us follow him. He swayed us with his brilliant oratory and mesmerized us with pageants and fireworks, he somehow managed to tap into our collective un—" (Eva kills the priest with one shot.)

"Go warm up the car, Otto, I'll be right with you." (Otto exits. Eva walks over to where a fur coat is hanging and removes it. She puts the coat over her slip and picks up a packed suitcase. She pauses. She puts it down. She places the gun in the hand of Hitler's corpse. She goes to the dresser and picks up a lighter. She pours some of the fluid on Hitler's body. She throws a match and flames begin to cover his body. She walks over and removes Hitler's mother Klara's picture from the wall, and throws it to the floor where it crashes. She calmly walks offstage as the audience goes nuts.)

20

Ball decided to get out before the crush. He walked down the deserted halls until he came to Becky's office. The door was open. He decided to sit down at Ickey's desk until it was time to return to the basement workshop. What? On top of Ickey's desk was a newsletter called *Lilith's Gang*, "a publication for feminists in the culture industry." On the first page was THE SEX LIST! Next to each male writer's name was a column that included the offense he'd committed. There were names of black as well as white male writers. He recognized some of the names. Floyd Salas. "Author of a poem entitled 'Pussy Pussy Everywhere,' in which he proposes that women lure men using furtive means." John A. Williams. "Author of book entitled, *! Click Song*, Tremonisha says that this book glorifies mixed marriages. Our people in subsidiary rights assure us that this book will never reach paperback." Cecil Brown. "Said in an article that 'there are as many female Hitlers as male Hitlers, and probably even more.' If he ever returns to the States we'll keep an eye on him." Next to Randy Shank and Jake Brashford's names was written "incorrigible." "Shank we understand is having hard times, but it will take time to reduce Brashford's reputation since he is supported by many aging white males of the modernist persuasion. They still have power, but within ten years most of them will be dead." He scanned the list for his name. Ian Ball. "Has shown improve-

ment after that terribly sexist *Suzanna*. He's also a southerner
and is not as bitter and as paranoid about women as some of
his northern soul brothers. With this issue we're removing him
from the sex list mainly as a result of Tremonisha's recommen-
dation." Ball almost leaped out of Ickey's chair, he was so
happy. If he had been close to Tremonisha at that moment he
would have hugged and kissed her.

He heard voices coming down the hall. *Eva's Honeymoon*
must have been almost over. He opened the door to Becky's
office part of the way, to see who was approaching. The old
lady was being helped down the hall by her chauffeur. If the
two had looked toward Becky's office they would have seen a
lone gray eye staring at them.

"I hope, madame, that this will be your last exercise in
folly," the chauffeur said.

"Oh, don't be angry with me, Otto," she said, patting the
arm that was aiding her. "I've always wanted the world to
know. To know my side. What really happened."

"But—"

"Don't worry, they can't trace it to me."

"It's just dangerous, madame, don't you think?"

"We've been together for forty years now. You can trust me.
I know that you couldn't trust the others, but you can trust
me. Trust me, Otto. This will be the last of my creative
efforts. I promise. I just couldn't resist the temptation to dance
on the grave of that son of a bitch. It's been forty years." They
walked past where Ball was standing behind the door. When
the coast was clear he headed down the stairs toward the basement where his workshop was probably ending. He stood outside the door, and heard Ham Hill's defense lawyer summing
up the defense for the jury.

"Something is wrong with Cora Mae. You see, white people
can't own you anymore, so they try to own you with their
eyes. They can't punch you anymore without getting harmed,
so they try to punch you with their eyes. They try to control

you. Nigger, what are you doing here, we don't want you here, they are saying to you with their eyes. Years ago it was the lynch rope. Now it's the rude stare. They look at you in airports, in restaurants. They stare at you like they're not used to anything." He could see some of the black women on the jury following Ball's directions ("as she is saying this the black jury members nod their approval"). "They've been accusing the blacks and Jews of owning the evil eye when they are the ones with the evil in their eyes. So here is this young boy, Ham Hill, minding his own business when this . . . this . . . vixen intrudes upon his space, glares at him with lust in her eyes, and when he pays no attention accuses him of reckless eyeballing, causing her husband and his friends to lynch the lad until he is dead." He could hear Cora Mae yell out, "No. It's not true."

"And twenty years after this child has been murdered, she comes along and says that what he did to her was similar to what her husband and that lynch mob did to Ham Hill. Now I ask you, ladies and gentlemen, isn't that the most air-headed thing you ever heard of?" Cora's attorney says, "I object, your honor." While the audience laughed, Ball walked away from the door and got a drink from the bartender, who was dressed in white jacket, black bow tie. He asked for a gin and tonic.

Who knows, he might luck up tonight, he thought. The bartender mixed his drink. "Looks like a hit, Mr. Ball. Congratulations." Ball smiled and sat at the stool of the bar, which had been set up in the lobby. He slowly imbibed. He could tell by the loud cheers and screams that the lawyer's speech was over. God, he was getting nervous. He went outside and walked around the block. When he returned he went back to the workshop space and listened in at the door. Cora Mae's lawyer was making her closing statement to the judge and jury.

"And when she felt his hot and dirty eyes on her she felt as though the scum of the world was taking an X-ray of her body. The men in this country think that all of the women are available to them, and so they use their eyes to scout in the same way that a predator stalks its prey. And though my distinguished opponent argues that Mr. Hill's only crime was that of having his eyes in the wrong place at the wrong time, I disagree. This man knew what his eyes were doing. He was raping her, in a manner of speaking, ladies and gentlemen. No, he didn't struggle with her or molest her with his hands; he did it with his eyes. He undressed her with his eyes. He accosted her with his eyes, he penetrated her with his eyes. He eye-raped her, ladies and gentlemen. For him, all she was was a cunt." Ball walked over to the bar and had another drink. He sat there for about ten minutes. Suddenly, there was wild applause mixed with a few boos. The people began to pour from the theater. They began to collect in the lobby and almost immediately the well-wishers came up and shook his hand, the ordinary black and white everyday people, that is. They had obviously enjoyed themselves. Even some feminists he'd seen on the art scene from time to time, including a few who'd given him problems in some of these little fly-by-night drama magazines, were congratulating him. The New York black avant-garde was leaning against the wall, grumbling, their jaws all tight. The men were dressed in an unorthodox way, anything to be different, and the women were wearing bizarre attire. There was this tall one who looked like she always wanted to fight and was always writing articles cussing white folks out, and would go up to Harlem and denounce the brothers who were with Anne—the American white woman—but next night she'd be in one of the downtown lesbian clubs dancing with Anne. The fellas said that this must have meant that she wanted to have all of the white women for herself. A bunch of backbiters and verbal scorpions, still back there with Malcolm X and John Coltrane when everybody knew that the greatest black militant they'd produced was Koffee Martin, who was from the South. Anyway, if they really wanted to embrace some politically far out position, let them go and mix it up with Pol Pot or the cynical and mean regime that runs Ethiopia.

This snit, who in his books was always dusting this politically incorrect person or that backslider and traitor, came toward Ball, leaving his group against the wall sulking. He rudely pushed through the crowd of well-wishers, and when he got to where Ball was standing he said: "White women elected Ronald Reagan, twice." Ball stamped his foot. The little fellow scampered back to his friends, to the amusement of the people who were gathered about Ball. A feminist came up and elbowed her way through the people who were telling him how great he was.

"Mr. Ball. I have an apology to make," she said.

"What apology, Ms.?"

"I was chairperson of women's studies at a small obscure university in Cincinnati and . . ." She broke down; it took a few seconds for her to regain her composure. "One of my stu dents wanted to write a dissertation on your plays and I—I."

"Go on," Ball said.

"I turned her down. I said that you were a notorious sexist even though I hadn't seen any of your work." Ball smiled and put his arm around her. She began crying on his chest.

"I understand," he said. "Sometimes we feel that our goals are so righteous, so necessary for the benefit of personkind, that we in our haste make mistakes that we later regret. Don't give it a second thought." The people gathered around murmured their approval. A woman whose shape revealed her to be a lover of animal fat and starches stepped forward.

"Me too, me too," she said. Ball and his admirers turned to her. "Do you remember a few years ago when you tried to get a one-acter staged at the theater I ran, and you got turned down? It was my fault. Now that I've seen *Reckless Eyeballing*, I feel so . . . so . . . I feel so bad." She too broke down and began sobbing like an infant. Ball had his arms about each in his attempt to console the two women. Suddenly a loud challenge came from the top of the stairs leading to the restrooms. "Ian. You ain't nothin' but a gangster and a con artist." It was Brashford—Ball and the people with him were shocked as Brashford began to descend the stairs. Uh oh, Ball thought. Brashford was going to imitate James Mason's drunken entrance in *A Star Is Born*. This classic beauty, a woman some would describe as "olive skinned," started up the stairs toward him and grabbed his arm. She was dressed in a black silk dress and wore some fine jewelry. She could not deter Brashford, who kept walking down the stairs and behaving like a Cossack in a *succoth*, as Isaac Babel would say.

"Tricking these people. You ain't nothin' but a trickologist with your fuzzy quick lines. You mischievous malicious bastard."

"Come on, dear," the woman said. He yanked his elbow from her grip and waved her away. "Ain't no way in the world for a jury to bring in a verdict of guilty against that corpse. In the version you gave me he's acquitted, after a confession from Cora Mae that she realized that she and the boy were in the same boat. Fellow sufferers. They made you change it. These vain, conniving bitches made you do it." The two feminists that Ball had been comforting glared at Brashford, and some of the patrons who remained to congratulate Ball looked at Brashford with utter disgust. The woman with Brashford said, "Dear."

"You keep out of it," he said. He wore a light blue suit that must have cost a grand and one of those Mike Hammer hats, which slid about his head as he came down the stairs. He also wore one of those British coats that intellectuals of the fifties favored. It was kind of like part of the existentialist's uniform. Camus wore one like it. It had shoulder straps, pockets, belts, and other features of little discernible use. A couple of Brashford's old-time liberal buddies, now neo-conservatives, who'd written little and had fallen hook, line, and sinker for the major intellectual, political and cultural trends of Europe only to be disillusioned time and again, started up the stairs to try to restrain their friend, the only colored in their club.

He punched the two, who already seemed out on their feet, and they fell down the stairs. The effort had placed Brashford off balance also, and he came tumbling down. Their friends helped them up, and Brashford sat up on the bottom stair, pulled a flask from his suit pocket, and took a long swig of something. He made a grunt, offending some of the first-nighters.

"I'm your literary father, you shit. And look at what you've done to me. A pitiful old man who has only one play to his name. But you wait. I'll show you. Wait until my masterpiece about the Armenians is staged. *Lengthy Struggle Toward the Borders of Darkness*. It's about this alcoholic father, see, with these two sons, who are real losers, and the mother, well she's a hophead and injects herself offstage—and . . . and . . ." Some of the people started to leave. Others shook their heads in sadness.

"These bitches had better not touch my play. Fucking twats. They hate the black man worst of all because they're sleeping with these other guys and are afraid to take a shot at them. Shit. Hey, that's not bad. I'm beginning to miss the old days when you were just hated because you were black." He began to laugh at his own joke. Others began to leave. He shouted after them.

"Hey. Where you going? Would you like to see a little ham bone?" He pulled up his trench coat and began to slap his thighs rhythmically. He began to sing some lewd choruses of the song "Mama Don't Allow," offending people with every dirty stanza. He finally reached the chorus: "Mama don't allow no *Playboy* reading in here/Mama don't allow no *Playboy* reading in here/We don't care what the Mama don't allow we going to read our *Playboy* anyhow," whereupon a few grim-faced feminists had stood all they were going to stand, and stormed out. A security guard finally came and told Brashford to leave. Brashford got up and tried to take a swing at the security guard, but the guard caught his arm, and brought it behind his back. The Mike Hammer hat fell to the floor. Somebody picked it up and followed the security guard and Brashford out of the theater. The people who had remained turned to Ball.

"This should be a night of victory, of triumph for me, but instead my heart is heavy. You all know how much I love Brashford. He befriended me after I wrote a long panegyric about him in the *Downtown Mandarin* in which I expressed my thanks to Brashford that the younger generation had such a fabulously endowed genius such as Jake to serve as our role model. That one play that he wrote, *The Man Who Was an Enigma*, though badly structured and containing some clumsy surrealistic passages and perhaps the most blatant example of author intrusion on record since the protagonist's life pretty much paralleled that of Jake's and in which the female characters are simply sexist and, well, I must have counted about forty mixed metaphors, served as a beacon for aspiring playwrights. But don't be so hard on Brashford for his behavior tonight. Remember him at his best as well as at his worst. Remember the good times as well as the bad. And don't be so hard on his generation. Those old men. All of their gods have failed, in a manner of speaking. As for what he said about me. Look, I've found that in this business people are going to say things and if I have raised antagonism, so be it, for that's what one gets when one tells the truth as one sees it." The two feminists who had wrongly attempted to censor his work cried even harder. They were embracing each other. From others came shouts of "hear, hear." There were congratulations all around. People were commenting on his magnanimity as they exited from the theater. He decided to take a little stroll backstage to see if the actors and actresses had left. There was one woman left. She had played Cora Mae's lawyer. She was undressing, and she had one foot up on a bench; she was removing her stockings and shoes.

"Oh, excuse me," he said.

"Oh, that's all right." She began pulling a dress over her slip. He had a chance to examine her hips, which didn't have any excess, and her legs—her beautiful legs. If she was a piano she'd probably be a Baldwin. A piano that his hands and fingers could, well, play beautiful music upon. She slipped into another dress. It was expensive and showed good taste. She turned to him and smiled when she saw him standing there, fascinated. They let their eyes do all of the talking and maybe later other parts of their anatomy would be communicating, that is, if he was lucky. The gin made him feel lucky. She finally said, "Aren't you going to the party?" The way she said it gave him a hard-on.

"I don't feel like partying. Just maybe going home and sacking out. Why don't you come over for a quick drink?" Sometimes they answer something that hurts your feelings, or they tell you that they had something else to do, but this was his night.

"Why not," she said. She had eyes like Judy Collins.

He took her home and fucked her until she was sore. Gin always affected him that way.

21

Lieutenant Brown slammed on the brakes and the police cars came to a screeching halt. "Loathesome" jumped from the car and ran up to Becky's apartment building. She was standing outside. She was in a white bathrobe and was wearing a towel about her head. She was still holding the gun. He took the gun from her and tried to talk to her and to calm her down.

"I think I hit him," she said. She pointed in the direction of Fifth Avenue. "Loathesome" headed in that direction. He saw drops of blood traveling in the same direction. He reached Fifth Avenue and turned the corner. A man in a beret and coat was leaning against the wall of a building; he was holding his side. He seemed to be in agony. O'Reedy gave chase. The man ran about a block and turned into an alley. It was about 3:00 A.M. and nobody was on the street. *Middle man, huh. Sean ought to see what I have to deal with. Creeps. Maniacs. Guys like this hair freak. I keep these freaks out of the public's hair. And do I get thanks. No. My own son . . .* He entered the dark alley. He slid against the wall, holding his gun. Nancy. Somebody hit him in the face. He felt something hard in his mouth. His teeth. His attacker wore a leather jacket, a leather beret, and a black mask. O'Reedy had the height and weight advantage over the man. He recovered in time to duck another blow. He licked some blood. The man was all over him, pummeling him. O'Reedy fell to the ground. All he could think of was that Tremonisha had gotten the Flower Phantom's description wrong. He was shorter. O'Reedy was taking quite a beating and was about to pass out when he heard his gun fall to the pavement. He became alert. The Flower Phantom grabbed the gun. He stood over O'Reedy. The three Spanish guys were at his side. They were folding their arms. They had big smiles. They were wearing some suits that had broad pointy shoulders, and pants that draped about their ankles. One wore a hat with a wide brim. Another was sporting a goatee. They wore shirts with exaggerated collars. They weren't wearing ties. The S.O.B.s weren't wearing ties! They moved to see O'Reedy looking down the barrel of Nancy. The Flower Phantom pulled the trigger. It didn't work. The Flower Phantom kept pulling the trigger; the same thing happened. In frustration, he threw the gun down. O'Reedy grabbed it and fired. The bullet missed the Flower Phantom's head by about two inches. The Flower Phantom started to run toward the other end of the alley. But he didn't get far. He was hit by a bullet that put a big hole in him, you could see through the hole to the wall across the street from the other entrance to the alley. He went up into the air and then slammed against the wall. O'Reedy could hear his ribs crack. He looked toward the direction of the gunfire. The jogger was standing— no, it was Lieutenant Brown. He was holding a shotgun.

"Everything okay, sir?"

He got up and went into the kitchen. The actress he'd brought home was still there. She was drinking some coffee. On the counter were two shopping bags with the name of the gourmet shop located around the corner from the hotel. Ball's postcoital manners were bad. He'd like whoever he'd balled the night before to clear out before dawn.

She looked good and probably went through tormenting exercises to remain that way. She looked to be about thirty-five. All of that gin. Her box was snug and fit him tight, and he kept saying O Jesus, and he wasn't even a religious man. She had sweet eyes set in a sweet face. She pushed a copy of *Hurry,* the weekly news magazine, across the table. He yawned. He looked at the picture on the cover. A man with long, black hair, the sort of forehead cut favored by writers Tom Wolfe and Frederick Douglass, and a frankfurter nose. He had a head like a California condor's. He resembled a young Charles Laughton—a young Charles Laughton in drag. He was standing next to a camera. The story read; CEZANNE OF THE CINEMA, and underneath in small letters was his quote: "*Wrong-Headed Man* Made Me Weep." She smiled as he looked over the cover.

"Towers Bradshaw, my husband," she said.

"The producer of *Wrong-Headed Man?*"

"Yeah," she said, sighing. "Only for him it's not just a movie. It has become a way of life. The Jews have their book, the Germans have their cathedral at Köln, the Egyptians their sphinx, he has his *Wrong-Headed Man.*" She was smart. He now liked that in women. Tremonisha had really changed him. He turned to the magazine inside where the story began. It showed another photo of him. She was standing behind him, of course. They were standing in front of a twenty-five-room Bel Air mansion, and five or six big cars were in the background. *Wrong-Headed Man* was getting to him all right. His eyes were glassy and he had about five days' growth on his chin. He appeared as though he hadn't gotten a good night's sleep in some time.

"The picture was taken on the day that I decided to leave him." In the photo she looked as though she'd already left. "He'd been up for a week reading *Wrong-Headed Man.* He'd wake me in the middle of the night, he'd be sweating and panting and he'd want me to read some lurid and sick passage from the book. During the session with the photographer he went into one of those crazy fits, you know, kind of like Jerry Lewis, and they had to call his mother to calm him down." He looked over at the basket on the kitchen table. It held what looked like French rolls. He walked over to the table, and yawned again. He hadn't bothered to put on a shirt. He wore

only a pair of jeans and sneakers. No socks, and no under-
pants. She stared at him for a moment. "I like your body," she
said. "How do you keep in such good shape?"

"I used to play soccer back home. I keep in shape over at
the Y. I swim." He sat down to a plate of different kinds of
cold cuts, some preserves, cheese, and coffee. There was
something curled up on the plate. He didn't like its looks.

"What's that?" he asked.

"Schmalz." It looked disgusting.

"This is a German breakfast, kind of like the kind we have
back at home in Freiburg," she said. So she was German. He
wondered why she kept saying what sounded like *kommen,
bitte, kommen, bitte,* all night long. She told him that she was
from Freiburg, a university town, and that in her twenties she
went to Berlin, where she hung out with filmmakers in
Kreuzburg, the Turkish section. She'd met *Wrong-Head's* producer at the Munich Film Festival where he'd come to be
honored for his first film, *Little Green Men.* She came to the
States with him. They were married. Since she left him she'd
been getting small parts in the New York theater. Before that
she'd appeared in her husband's films. She was always getting
mutilated or decapitated. In one, she was dismembered by a
chainsaw.

"I still don't know what he saw in the film. It was so unlike
him to take on a project like that." He did science fiction plots
that were so embellished with special effects that you forgot the
weak story lines and the bad acting. "I mean, I agreed with the
main character's point of view, I think, but I thought that
some of the situations were, well, morbid. She doesn't seem to
offer any alternative to fucking men, and that lesbian business
seemed to be really a tease. But, of course, I'm white." She
was dark and Mediterranean looking, probably from Bavaria,
he thought. A G.I. had told him that he'd seen Italians with
black faces and kinky hair in Frankfurt, and in the German
south the people looked like mulattoes.

"What do you think of *Wrong-Headed Man?*" she asked.

"In my opinion, a woman who puts urine and spit into her guests' drinks deserves what happens to her." They laughed.

"Do you want some more coffee?" She started for the counter where the sterling silver coffeemaker—a gift from his mom— stood. When she came by him he pulled her to him. She sat on his lap. She was wearing a thin dress and he could feel her in his lap. She kissed him for a long time. He put his hand inside her dress and felt her ass. She pulled away and headed toward the counter for the coffee.

"He and Tremonisha have had a falling out, I hear," she said.

"First she dragged this actress in to play the missionary who had no acting ability at all, but Tremonisha insisted. She got the role over all of the other talented black actresses." He looked at the schmalz. He decided that he wasn't going to have any of it. He could see the stuff lying all fat and sluggish in his arteries.

"Do you know the actress?" she asked. No, he didn't know her, but the fellas had said that to compare her with Butterfly McQueen would be an insult to Ms. McQueen.

"Then he threw out her script."

"Yeah, I heard about that," he said.

"She threatened him with a lawsuit."

"What did he do?" She came back and set the coffee next to his plate. She walked back to her chair at the other end of the small table. She sat down and cut a roll in two and spread some jam on one half. He looked up at his poster of Bugs Bunny, his favorite cartoon character.

"He owned the film and so he cut off all contact with her. He forgot that Tremonisha even wrote it. Kept calling it his play. His film. He's been working on it for a year now. He'll never finish it." The magazine called the film his greatest challenge. "I hear that when he's not working on it he dresses up in that adventurer's suit and makes believe that he's Joe

Beowulf. He spends the day tooting up his nose and playing computer games," she said. Joe Beowulf was a swashbuckling white man that he'd created. He went about the world slapping women left and right and bringing Third World people to their knees. He remembered the ad carried in the newspapers. It showed Joe Beowulf in a camouflage suit and a machine gun in hand. Lurking in the background were the illustrator's version of black muggers. The illustrator thought that blacks still wore Afros. "Fighting the Grendels of this World," said the copy that accompanied the photo.

"Guy sounds like he has a lot of problems. Why did you marry him?"

She paused, and shifted her weight before saying, "Guilty, I guess."

"Let's go down to McDonald's," he said.

"But you just—"

"Yeah. I like your German breakfast, but I lost a lot of protein last night, I need some food."

"Let me get my coat." She went into the bedroom. He finished his cup of coffee. German coffee tasted like Maxwell House. He turned to the article again. The one about the filming of *Wrong-Headed Man*. The magazine said that the film had something to do with "incest, sexual brutality, and Sapphic love." He looked up the word, Sapphic. The dictionary said that it had something to do with dykes.

After breakfast, he went back to his apartment to read the newspaper. He was still a little woozy from the gin and exhausted from fucking all night.

The morning's headline hit him in the face like Boom Boom Mancini. "FLOWER PHANTOM SLAIN." He scanned the column, trying to focus upon the important details. A man identified as Randy Shank was slain a few blocks from the apartment of Becky French, after the suspect attempted to enter her apartment from a fire escape, located next to her window. Randy Shank was a black playwright who had achieved some notoriety in the 1960s. Detective Lawrence O'Reedy pursued the man through the East Village and foiled his attempt to make good on his threat to "get" Becky French for her support of Tremonisha Smarts' stand on castration for perpetrators of rape. Ms. Smarts, whose play *Wrong-Headed Man* received international recognition, was Shank's first victim. At the time, the suspect told Ms. Smarts that he was patterning his actions after those of the French Resistance who shaved the heads of women who collaborated with the Nazis. Experts claimed that Mr. Shank, who became known as the Flower Phantom for his bizarre habit of leaving a chrysanthemum with his victims, was suffering from a paranoid fantasy and that instead of being the political hero he desired to be was actually a hair fetishist. This was shocking to Ball. He had to regain his composure. The phone rang. It was Becky French. He asked her was she all right. She said her only regret was that she'd used a .22 instead of a .44. She said that if she'd used a .44 they'd still be cleaning up his intestines. Ball cleared his throat.

"The reason I called is because I have some good news. We're taking your play to Broadway. Several producers have expressed interest. We have to see which one will give us the best deal. Perhaps you realize now why it was important to change the play so that Cora Mae's viewpoint condemned both Ham and his lynchers. That one can be murdered by reckless eyeballing just as easily as with a weapon. It's the same thing. Congratulations, Ian. I never told you this, but after Jim came up missing I wasn't even going to give you a workshop, but Tremonisha argued on your behalf. You owe her one, Ball. You'll be pleased to know that now you'll be able to work anywhere in this town." Ball jumped up from the table where he was having breakfast. Broadway. People in mink coats arriving from the suburbs. Chartered buses in front of the theater. Interviews. Women. Gol-lee, he said to himself. He was becoming "bankable." Producers would be lining up. Three-hour lunches. Talk shows. *People* magazine. Parties. If only Chester Himes and Jake Brashford were less controversial, more amiable, more toned down. If only they had cooled it. They could have had all of this too.

He dialed Brashford's number. He wanted to tell him the good news. He was sure that Brashford had gotten over his hangover by now. He identified himself to the speaker on the other end. A woman.

"Oh, yes. I saw you last night. I was with my husband." So the woman with what James Fenimore Cooper called "tartar cheeks" was Brashford's wife. "He's really sorry for the way he behaved. He said that he will make it up to you somehow. He was really not himself. The lawyers have gone down to bail him out of jail."

"Jail?"

"Yes. After the security guard took him outside, Jake managed to get free. He knocked the security guard cold with one punch. Then the police arrived. He got into a slugging match with the officers. I've never seen him like that. It all started at dinner. He went through three bottles of wine. The reason we were only able to catch the last act of your play is because he spilled the wine on his pants in the restaurant and then had to go home and change. When he got to his studio he started to drink again and went into some anti-Semitic tirade, which is what always happens when he's drunk or feeling sorry himself. It's crazy because I'm Jewish and he has a Jewish son. I think it's the play that's making him this way. He's trying to write a play of universal values, but everywhere he turns, he runs into ethnicity. For twenty years he's been hopping from group to group. He must have tons of discarded drafts in his closet. For the last year it's been the Armenians, now he's talking about doing the Jews. He's so depressed these days, Ian. He's so lonely. He's like the trumpet player in that movie *Young Man with a Horn* who was seeking the ultimate high note. For

Brashford that high note is universality. It keeps eluding him. The blacks of his generation avoid him and the younger generation has never heard of him." I'm hip to that, Ball thought.

"Of course, Ms. Brashford—"

"You can call me Delilah."

"And you can call me Ian, Ms. Brashford. Don't you worry about my abandoning Jake. Why, he's my Immamu, my guide, my shaman, and my guru. Ms. Brashford, Jake is, well, like a father to me. Everything I know, I learned from him. He taught me how to survive in this city, me, a poor country boy. I'll always be grateful, and Delilah, where I come from the saying goes you love your friends and you hate your enemies."

"That's so sweet of you, Ian. Jake always told me that you were his best friend."

"Did he say that, Delilah?"

"He says it all the time. He'll probably talk to you when he returns from abroad, Ian. We're leaving as soon as he's out of jail. I think that we need a vacation. We both agree that he needs a change of scenery. He says that on some days he just feels like taking his four volumes of Malraux, his Duke Ellington records, his Motherwells, and his *Complete Plays of O'Neill* and going to live in a coal bin."

"Where do you plan to go?"

"We're leaving tomorrow for Tel Aviv."

It had been a dense morning for Ian.

Jim, Randy Shank, and now Brashford. Jim thought that the whole country was like New York and as soon as he left Manhattan he wandered into an obeah zone. The wrong neighborhood. Lost in the night. Randy Shank, appropriate that his ending came as it did. Sometimes he was the son of a gun, a loud, belligerent, talking hot dog, but his real bullet was a flower, as evidenced in his early poetry, lyrical, tender. Driven from Europe by Tremonisha and Johnnie Kranshaw's badmouthing, marked as a man who would go to any lengths for sex. Brashford, isolated, yammering about the theft of black culture by the Jews, condemned to wander from ethnicity to ethnicity until he was left with the very group he roiled against. Maybe these city guys were right about him, Ball thought. Maybe he was acceptable because he was from the South and therefore viewed as a genteel and "slow-to-anger" person. Those northern blacks had reputations all over the hemisphere as those who would stand for no gunk. But no one was listening to them anymore. The people in the United States were tired of hearing about their apartheid and so imported the apartheid from abroad. They sent relief money to Africa without so much as a glance at the thirty million or so who went to bed at night hungry in the U.S. So audiences applauded *Master Harold and the Boys* because this was about somebody else's apartheid and they could laugh and attend matinees because nobody was pointing the finger at them. Maybe he was just another insouciant import. Maybe they felt that as a Southerner he would look back to the old days when the darkies articulated their words very slowly and carefully. How did that ad for Jamaica put it: "Come back to the way things used to be," uttered by an old black man, beckoning. It didn't bother Ball what reasons were given for pushing him, he just wanted success, as his second-sighted mother used to say, "Boy, your eyes are bigger than your belly." And what about Tre, and the rest of America's black sisters? He could understand their bitterness, and their hurt. Extras in a land where Anne—the American white woman—had the leading role, her smiling face on the products, the covers of magazines, the ubiquitous face (it was the 1980s and the demand for black models was now on the decrease, while that for Swedish types was on the increase). It was miraculous that so many were able to maintain their poise and their sanity and not go off the deep end like Toni Case Bambara's Velma, who had to "undergo a riding." Velma, who got so fed up with the boy-men in her life that she growled. The black women were objects of scorn and desire, like Toni Morrison's Sula, who wanted to be

free as any man, in a time when a woman who smoked cigarettes or sat in bars was regarded as a witch. If sometimes the
fellas viewed some of them as hostile, perhaps their hostility
was merely a defense mechanism.

He could understand Clotel, getting it from both sides, neither black nor white but Anne and Coretha in one. And what
about Anne? What if women were harming themselves, muti-
lating themselves, and risking bad health to look like you? The
black ones, ninety percent of whom risked baldness by straightening their hair? The Asian ones having the slants removed
from their eyes by plastic surgery, and the doctors rearranging
the bones of the Jewish women's noses with mallets. No wonder Becky was so haughty, so demanding, and so full of herself. People were undergoing torture in order to look like her.
He could understand the women, Ball could, and Tre had
taught him to communicate to a woman without having to
devise tedious strategies for getting them into bed. Tre had
taught him that there was more to a woman than a cunt.
Much more.

But on the other hand, suppose Cecil Brown was right when
he said that there are probably more female Hitlers than male.
That got Ball to thinking. Weren't women the ones who were
always interested in what was going on in their neighbors' intimate existence, like the Mouth Almighties in *Their Eyes Were
Watching God?* Weren't they the ones who rummaged their
children's possessions, and went through their husband's
pockets? Weren't they the gossips? Hadn't some of the feminists said that what went on in your house was also political?
Suppose they gain power. Would they send people into your
house to see what you were doing in there? Go through your
pockets, spy on your children? Were women more fascistic
than men? Was this why men wanted to get away, like a pris-
oner escaping from some domestic Devil's Island? The North,
Ball decided, was one hell of a complicated mess. That's why
it fascinated him so; his mother complained that he was trying

to become more northern than the Northerners, with his video cassettes, comic books, Coca-Cola, rock-and-roll records, baseball. Ball called the airlines to reconfirm his reservation that afternoon. He would pick up the reviews in the airport. He couldn't wait to get South.

23

The commissioner pinned the medal on O'Reedy's chest to the sound of enthusiastic applause. A few people got up from their seats, and soon the entire gathering of police was on its feet applauding "Loathesome" O'Reedy, who was retiring from the police force after thirty years' service. Somebody had placed pots of yellow flowers on each side of the lectern and alongside the place where the dignitaries sat was a large American flag. Larry's wife was standing next to him. She was in tears. She wore a large corsage and had her hair tinted blue for the occasion. She wore white gloves. She was dressed in what some irreverents dubbed Mamie Eisenhower pink. As soon as the applause subsided some rookies in the rear of the auditorium began to chant: "Give me something to write home to Mother about, Give me something to write home to Mother about," the line O'Reedy had always shouted before giving some creep his Kingdom Come. O'Reedy put out his hand, a signal for the rookies to stop. The only noise that remained was made by the shuffling of feet and some coughing. O'Reedy approached the speaker's stand. "I've been thinking about

this day for thirty years now. What I would say on the occasion of my retirement. You all know how hard it is to be a cop.
People don't know how hard it is. The murder and the mayhem we see. We see human beings behaving like animals, and
it's tough to take. After a while you get to thinking that maybe
that's what we are. I'm not saying that we're apes or nothin'
like that." His line was interrupted by a flurry of giggles.
"Well, you know what I mean. It's just that in this business
you learn that there's no difference between man and the
lowliest beast you find in the jungle. You try to do your best."
A lone voice yelled, "Give me something to write home to
Mother about." The shout was followed by more giggles, then
the entire room was chanting again, "Give me something to
write home to Mother about." O'Reedy quieted the audience
again. "But seriously, folks, animal or no animal, we showed
these punks that they can't take the streets from us, and though
our methods were a little unorthodox"—the audience rose as
one and applauded wildly for about two minutes. After the
applause died down this time, the audience spent some more
seconds agreeing with O'Reedy's statement and nodding their
heads in approval, "I guess I'm a lucky guy. I have a good
wife." Mrs. O'Reedy was hesitant to stand but the audience's
applause was so unstinting that the police commissioner encouraged her to stand and take a bow. O'Reedy walked over
and kissed his wife, as the audience continued its applause and
whistled. "Got a great kid, too, has a head on his shoulders,
not like this dumb cop you see standing before you; he's going
to study Irish-Americans . . . ah . . . you know, that's about
how great we Irishmen are, which a lot of you bozos don't
appreciate. Stand up, son." Sean rose and bowed all around.
"Well, I thought—what the hell—back there a few months
ago that my retirement would be uneventful, but I guess you
all read the papers last night about what happened." The audience went ape. They started laughing and some cried, and
people were chanting, "Give me something to write home to

Mother about." "And I tell you what," he said after they finished, "I would have been a goner had it not been for Lieutenant Brown. Stand up, Lieutenant." Another huge ovation, and some of Brown's colleagues razzed him with "Way to go, Brown." "The women of this city can wake up this morning with the knowledge that at least one creep won't be around to make their lives miserable and cause them to live in a state of fear. I was against Brown, the other blacks, the Hispanics, and the women coming on the force. You know how hard it is for an old guy like me to change, but you know, now that they're here I'm wondering, hey, how did we get along without them all these years," he said, his voice cracking with emotion. The Hispanics and blacks and women cheered, and about ten percent of the white males applauded too. "Well, you guys won't have Larry O'Reedy to kick around anymore, me and the missus are leaving for Vero Beach tomorrow, and I'm not going to do anything for the rest of my life but fish and sit on my can and watch the ball game." O'Reedy smiled at the new round of applause that he was getting.

He looked at the domed ceiling. He stepped back. Stopped talking. People in the audience began to whisper. The ceiling was blank but he saw an ascension mural with a lot of browns reds blues and whites. His eyes were wide open as he stood there, fascinated by what he saw. The black jogger was floating in his black and red jogging suit, his hands thrust in front of him floating toward heaven—and all of the other people were off their feet, floating also, all of them ascending behind the jogger, and there was the Amazon who had laid down her sword and removed her helmet and she was ascending, and his relatives; his Mom and Dad, they were folding their hands and they were ascending together, and everybody was looking heavenward, and there were people in chariots pulled by snorting horses, and he recognized dead aunts and uncles, his grandparents rising, and those three Spanish guys, don't forget the three Spanish guys, they were also in robes and wore wings, and some kind of Mexican hats, and one of them was playing the saxophone. And there they were, also ascending, and some little black and Puerto Rican babies with puffy cheeks and diapers and wings were blowing little trumpets.

He started running toward the ceiling and he was flying toward the others who were leaving him behind and he was shouting "Wait for me, wait for me." He staggered across the stage, and as he did he saw his wife's mouth open and the police commissioner show a frown of concern, and his hands went up as he staggered across the stage floating in slow motion, and trying to grab on to the American flagpole, but he missed it and fell off the stage. He heard the screams.

He came to momentarily. Sean, his son, was lifting his head. Somebody was giving him a glass of water. The police commissioner was on his feet telling others to "Get back! Get back!"

"I—did you see."

"Don't try to talk, dear," his wife said. She was kneeling next to him. He took her hand.

"I guess I won't be gettin' to Vero Beach."

"Dad, take it easy, they've sent for an ambulance."

"Yeah." He smiled. He tried to rise, but he couldn't. He looked up at his wife. "You've been so great to me, and I've been like a—a—I stink—I had my whores."

"Please, dear, we'll talk about it, try to keep still."

He looked at Sean. "I'm sorry about that . . . tell me about this guy James T. Farrell, you say he could write, huh."

"The best. He wrote a novel about an Irish-American guy named Studs Lonigan. A real loser."

"Kind of like me, huh. Studs Lonigan."

"No, Dad. Studs was a victim of change."

"The insurance is all paid," O'Reedy said, interrupting his son and turning to his wife. "It's in the chest I keep in the closet, it . . ." A sharp pain hit O'Reedy in the abdomen. He groaned. He could hear the ambulance in the distance.

"Sean, you're right . . . I was their errand boy—I didn't have nothin' against niggers and Puerto Ricans. Those were evil men, Sean. It's not the old days. . . . If we don't stop them, Sean . . . They're having babies. Sean, you don't understand. You have to see some of the stuff I've seen, Sean, I'm right there at the front lines and it ain't pretty—maybe that black guy who was running . . . Sean, sometimes you can't tell them apart, just a lot of faces staring at you, hating you. . . . Sean, we're doing this for you, we're in the trenches, you'll see." O'Reedy looked up. He saw clouds, the bottom of the feet and the skirts of the people in the mural, flying, heading toward the sky like the murals in churches overseas, ascending, like the cathedral at Köln looming over the city like some kind of regal but ragged, nasty and dirty pigeon, flying. But a figure was heading toward him. It was O'Reedy, the black jogger who had the same name as his; he was coming back, and he hovered above the people standing around O'Reedy, his wings connected to the black and red jogging suit, and O'Reedy lifted himself and touched the jogger's outstretched finger with his.

He was a passenger in one of those Air France hot rods and they were rattling into New Oyo, about two hours from leaving St. Thomas in the Bahamas. When they landed he saw from the plane's window a huge banner in front of the building that housed the control tower. "Ian Ball, Welcome Home, Our Own," written in the language of the island. The other passengers stared at him as he walked down the steps of the plane. A small brass band was there to welcome him. They played the New Oyo anthem. They were dressed in white uniforms with gold trimmings. His fellow passengers had to go through customs to have their passports checked and their luggage searched. Two officers from the government introduced themselves and escorted him through customs and toward the car the president of New Oyo had sent. Later he learned that his mother had requested this greeting from the president of New Oyo, who was one of her best customers. He believed in soothsaying and the other services his mother provided to well-placed people. The president always credited his mother with having saved his life after she had warned him of an assassination plot against him.

He and the escorts headed toward the outside of the airport; they were carrying his bags. There was a disturbance. He wheeled to the source of the loud, drunken singing. His escorts froze. There were some Americans, Club Med types who were doing a conga line at the ticket counter as they checked in for the trip back to the States. They were wearing shorts and had the usual obnoxious, know-it-all attitude one associates with American travelers. They were singing the tune to "God Bless America," but without the usual lines: "No more roosters/crowing all night/no more cockroaches/in the bread. God Bless America/all the mosquitoes there are dead/God Bless America, I'm going home, to bed."

He and his escorts exited through the doors. He saw vending machines containing the nation's newspapers. His face was on their covers. One headline said: I. BALL TO BROADWAY. Some people driving by in their Fiats and B.M.W.s and Mercedes honked. News traveled fast down here.

He'd picked up the reviews of the play at J.F.K. and read them on the plane. The sex list with his name crossed out must have made the rounds, because the feminist critic for the

New York Exegesis, the big paper, had given it a rave review. She called it "riveting," "brilliant," and one of the most "memorable" plays of the season. He received only two paragraphs less than *Eva's Honeymoon* in the *Downtown Mandarin*. Near the bottom of the second page was a head that read: SHOBOATER'S VIEW. His review was carried way in the back. Page sixty-eight.

"*Reckless Eyeballing* is marred by flat characters, but that's not the worst offense that Ian Ball has committed in this piece of rubbish. Mr. Ball has a way of talking out of both sides of his mouth, as though he were of two heads or of two minds. When misogyny was in, he wrote *Suzanna*, the play about the sugar cane worker who regularly took the cutters into the fields in order to pay her gambling debts and buy rum. Although the women were outraged by this slut, at least Ball knew what he was writing about. *Reckless Eyeballing* is an obvious attempt to distance himself from the misogynistic attitudes that have ruined the work of some of his contemporaries. It's all things for all women. He gives the black women the good debating points; he gives the white women the victory by having the all-female jury (the only male character in the entire play is Ham Hill's skeleton) return a verdict against the corpse, Ham Hill, who was lynched twenty years before for allegedly gazing too long at Cora Mae, a white woman. Ball even lets the corpse off by having the judge sentence him to death already served. If Ian Ball was as good a playwright as he is a cunning opportunist, and a flexible equivocating and ambitious knave, maybe he would deserve the overpraise that this play is bound to receive."

He ignored the review by Paul Shoboater, and doubted whether many readers would accept his view, that is, if they could locate it in the newspaper. What counted was the review he'd received from the feminist critic on the front page. A letter from Tremonisha had arrived, just as he was leaving his apartment for the airport.

"Dear Ian," it began. "Greetings from Yuba City, California. I was looking for the worst town in the United States. This is it. I'm sorry I left you stranded, Ian, but I think that if I had remained in New York, I would have lost my mind. I just couldn't be a party to what Becky did to your play. She reminds me of "that woman in Hampstead," you know, that conniving spidery creature in Paula Marshall's novel. Attempting to control those around her by dangling the golden apple of artistic success. Did I ever tell you that I saw Johnnie Kranshaw a couple of weeks before she disappeared? She had been up for a week and had so much coke in a bowl that I mistook it for sugar and started to put it into my coffee. She was haggard and smelly. She looked eighty years old. Becky had sucked her insides out. I've gotten three thousand miles between me and that whole New York scene and I don't miss a thing.

"Dred Creme is with me. He's been off junk for about five weeks now. Next I'm going to get him to work on those other bad habits of his. Sucking his thumb and holding this blanket next to his head all the time. He's practicing his scales. He says that he knew he was playing bullshit and drowning in clichés in New York. He's listening to Jelly Roll Morton and says he wishes that he'd heard of him and King Oliver when he was in his late thirties.

"The sun is doing wonders for him. We're happy and we're thinking about getting married and raising some kids. New York was no place to raise kids. Anyway, remember that night I just about talked your ears off about the Jew in *Jud Süss*? I've been thinking a lot lately of what happened in one scene. You see, this Jew gets rid of his caftan and his beard, and shows up at this party, see, and he thinks that because he has the Amadeus look, that the Germans will accept him; but no, a blond stereotype of the heroic German says, pointing to him, 'You a Jew ain't you.' And so maybe that's what's happened to me. I thought that by getting rid of the caftan and beard of my experience, the people I admired would accept me. As a result, I became something I'm not.

"You know, we didn't get into this black thing until late. When I was a kid my sisters and I told everybody that we were Cuban; black was ugly. Then when black came in I became that, and when the feminist thing was the hip lick I joined that and then the womanist fad. I was trying to please the sisterhood, and even attended these seminars where people discussed whether the clitoral orgasm would be replaced by the vaginal kind. That is, when they were not talking about the Grafenberg spot. Back here in Yuba City I'm trying to get back to where I started from. I grew up in a town like this. I went to the best schools, came out, belonged to the Jack and Jills and went away to college to be accepted as the first black girl in one of the most exclusive sororities.

"One of my teachers encouraged me to write plays and some of them were staged by the college drama department. Then I won that national playwrighting contest. After that it was off to New York, and, well, the rest is, as they say, history. I staged my play *Wrong-Headed Man* in one of the East Village bars. Becky saw it and got me the Mountbatten. The success of *Wrong-Headed Man* turned into my curse. You know what those brothers said about me, and even some of the black women were hostile. I didn't care. What money or influence did they have? Besides, no matter how vanguard they thought they were—those intellectuals and artists downtown—they were still impressed by somebody who made it big. Got their picture in *People* magazine. I was whisked away into the Broadway lights, I was wide-eyed like Judy Garland in *The Wizard of Oz*, everything was so unreal; the parties, the interviews, being in the same room with people you'd only read about, people who were legends, people telling me how much they liked my play. Then the questions. Some of the questions they asked were, well, sick. They didn't bother me at first because I had convinced myself that their praise was genuine. But they kept asking these questions.

"I was writing about some brutal black guys who I knew in my life who beat women, abandoned their children, cynical, ignorant, and arrogant, you know these types, but my critics and the people who praised me took some of these characters and made them out to be *all* black men. That hurt me. The black ones who hated me and the white ones who loved me were both unfair to me. Nobody takes the crude and hateful white men like Hoss and Crow in Sam Shepard's plays and says that these men represent all white men. Has anybody ever said that Richard III represented all white men? That all white men craved to lock children in a tower somewhere for perverse reasons? Nobody ever said Lady MacBeth or Medea represented all white women. That all white women manipulated their husbands into committing acts of murder or desired to murder their children. I thought they were my fans, those feminists, but some of them would have drinks and ask me about the 'raw sex' and how black men were, you know. Others used my black male characters as an excuse to hate all black men, especially some of these white women. Then they wouldn't feel so guilty for taking their jobs. I was making this money and getting all of this praise when in reality I was no better than one of those panderers you see in the live sex shows up in North Beach. I was like a proprietor of one of those nasty adult movie houses you find in the rude sections of Cleveland and Rochester, where for a quarter you can go see a woman fuck a dog. With the feminists on my side and the support of those white males who had some strange passion for black men, I could have stayed in New York, but I left. Like Frank Sinatra says, I was at 'the top of the heap,' but the heap stinks, and I left before they could toss me into the shit. I think I'm just going to stay here in Yuba City. It doesn't even have bus service. There is no airport. No colleges, universities, no theaters or symphonies. The average household income is under thirty thousand dollars. It doesn't even have a bowling lane, but all I need at this point are my memories and a library. Yuba City has twelve. I'm just going to get fat, have babies, and write write write.

"And I'm going to take your advice, too. You're right. What did you say Jake Brashford called it? Finishing school lumpen. I knew that people who were aware would see through my dumb attempt to be down. Though the critics and the white feminists fell for it, I knew that those working class characters that I tried to write about and their proletariat voices I attempted to mime were phony. All of us who grew up in the middle class want to romanticize people who are worse off than we are. And suppose as Nikki said, and she was right, that some of these teenage welfare mothers started to really try to use that time they have to cultivate their children instead of partying, doing the freaky deaky, and spending the diaper money on reefer. Take them to museums and work with them on their reading. It won't be long before some of these teenage mothers will begin writing about places like Bed-Stuy themselves, and then all of us debutantes will have to write about ourselves, will have to write about our backgrounds instead of playing tour guides to the exotics.

"There's probably somebody in jail right now who's writing a book that will put our little artsy ghetto plays out of business and make them seem innocuous. Anyway, I've begun a new play. You remember how you guys got on me because I went on TV that time and said that when black men weren't killing each other, they were killing women. Well, I was wrong and you were right. It's the other way around, according to statistics. The women are the ones who are killing the men, and they get off too, as though there were some kind of bounty on black men. In my new play I tell the truth, and I know Becky and her friends will write me off after it's produced. It's about a woman who leaves her husband for another woman only to discover that she's a batterer. See, this is a problem that the male-loathing feminists don't want to discuss: women beating up on women. It's an epidemic, and the women's shelters are full of women who are fleeing other women. Yes, men should stop beating up women, and women have to stop beating up women, too. And men and women must stop killing each other. The feminists don't want to bring up these taboo subjects because they feel it will hurt their cause. Well, if they're afraid to tell the truth because they feel that it will play into the hands of their enemies, then their enemies have won. Same thing with the Jews and the blacks. If they are afraid to tell the truth for fear of furnishing ammunition to their enemies or if they're trying to deflect legitimate criticism by dismissing it as anti-Semitic, or racist, then the Nazis will have won and the Klan will have won, and all of the other bigots under the sheets, and setting fires to synagogues will have won. Boy, I sure have put a bug in your ear, so I guess I will end this letter. Dred Creme is lying in my lap, he's been practicing all day and I just gave him some warm milk and am about to put him to bed. Tomorrow's his birthday and I'm going to take him to the circus. Take care, Ian, and who knows, one day you'll answer your door down there on that beautiful island of yours and you'll see Dred Creme and me standing there with our bags—"

I hope not, Ian thought. He got into the back of the Citroën that his mother had sent for him. The chauffeur started to gibber something in that inscrutable creole the poorer classes of people spoke on the island. "Shut up, you black monkey," Ian said in the mother tongue, a signal that he didn't want to be disturbed. The car passed through the city of narrow streets and houses, which resembled the style of those in New Orleans. It passed the market place where the women were selling fruit and vegetables that were so large they could have been entered in the *Guinness Book of Records*, or Ripley's Believe It or Not. The black women down here walked with their hips swinging and sat in the market with their legs apart. Up north there was the wizened hoary Protestant white father god brought to North America by the Puritans who looked after things, but down here it was Mama. Island and water deities. The love had some spice to it, the sex was piping hot, and the sun made you drunk. On one side of the island was the Caribbean, soft, peaceful, coated with specks of light from the sun, but on the other side was the killer Atlantic. Two things that blacks all over the Americas had phobias about: the Atlantic, bloodhounds.

Soon the car was leaving the city where castles and hovels existed alongside one another and moving out into the country. On one mountain stood a bronze statue of Koffee Martin, the national hero. On another mountain in the distance he could see the Shoboater estate where Paul's family lived in the style of the colonialists. Once in a while, Paul's father could be seen in town. He was a very fair-skinned man who dressed like Noël Coward and used a walking stick, and did things for the queen of the Mother Country. They drove for about forty-five minutes until they came to his mother's spacious home and lawns. He walked up the steps, the chauffeur following him, carrying his bags. His mother came out and opened her arms. They embraced for a long time.

The maid was the color of carbon paper. She curtsied as Martha Ball and her son entered the house. Some members of the household staff were also present, and they greeted him as copiously as the first maid had. One of the boys—a man who must have been in his early fifties—took his bags upstairs. "Well," she asked, "did you bring them?"

"I didn't forget, Ma," he said, taking the record albums from a bag and handing them to her. They were by Tina Turner. His mother and her friends were crazy about Tina Turner, way down here, and come to think of it his mother did resemble Tina Turner, full in the thighs, her hair worn down the sides of her face, and the kind of lips that you get when you cross an Arawak and a Congolese.

"Boy, you know how much I love that girl. The United States, they may be how you say, *Rehob*, but they produce Tina Turner. A red woman like us." She placed the albums on a hall table. The fellas had said that Ms. Turner's song

"Private Dancer" symbolized the bond between white men and Third World women all over the Americas. It was their love anthem.

"Your dinner will be coming soon." He'd eaten on the airplane but he knew that she'd have to have her way. She always had her way. There was no arguing with her. He knew that he would have to eat again.

"I have a surprise for you," she frowned. "Boy, why you wearin' that black leather jacket, those jeans and what are those, cowboy boots?" She looked down at his boots. "Who you tryin' to be, Roy Rogers? You done gone to the United States. You done become an American." She wished that he would come home. Her friends in government would give him an ambassador's post. Many literary men down here were ambassadors, mayors. She wanted him to leave New York. He could even become a banker in one of the overseas banks. Chase Manhattan.

"I may live in the United States, Ma, but my soul is here, my very character was formed by New Oyo."

"Go on with ya. You have a tongue like your—" She started to say it. All of these years she'd resisted the temptation to tell him the secret. One day she would. They came to the end of the long hall with its hardwood floors, its high ceilings, the vases of flowers placed on tables, the autographed portraits on each wall. Everything was gleaming. Presidents, senators, literary figures, great artists. Some said that she actually influenced the policies of the nation through every president who'd been elected, since they were all believers.

They walked into the dining room with its view of the Caribbean and mountains gingerly touched by clouds. On the slopes of one he could see some goats grazing. A woman was standing with her back to them staring out of the window. She was enjoying the view and held a glass of champagne in her hand. She turned around. He recognized her from her pictures. It was Johnnie Kranshaw. She was very dark and had what some called "dancing eyes." She wore her hair short and was wearing what some called an "African dress," though it didn't have the splashy colors of the native women, nor the overstated jewelry. Ms. Kranshaw was a Protestant, all right.

"Ms. Kranshaw. I've heard a lot about you," he said when his mother introduced them. That he had. The fellas said that if she hadn't been born the white man would have invented her and other vile and terrible things.

"Your reputation precedes you, Mr. Ball. I read the review in the international edition of the *Herald Tribune*. Looks as if you have a hit."

"We think so," he said. They sat down for dinner, and the girl brought out the oxtail soup. She served on her right instead of on the diner's left. Martha Ball issued a quick insult. Called the girl a black idiot in the language of the Mother Country. The maid stared dumbly and began to serve from the left. Martha was a stern disciplinarian and was always complaining about how hard it was to keep good household servants. About a third of the youth who lived in this little country town had left for the city, where the unemployment rate was staggering, while still others had traveled overseas to the Mother Country where they were stealing and pimping like every other first generation of immigrants who find themselves subject to hostile treatment and who are barred from the legitimate ways of earning money.

Though some would have us believe that the Italian-, Irish-, and Jewish-Americans went from Ellis Island to comfort without no in-between, in their poor days they could match any black "underclass" statistic for statistic. The writers who tell the truth about those Hell's Kitchen and Lower East Side days are unwelcome. Mike Gold is neglected; he reminds them of the time when they didn't have a pot to piss in. The warts of black Americans were right there for everybody to see and even close-upped in the mass media that harassed them; other groups applied a lot of makeup to theirs. Martha was upset about the youth and often talked to the president about it. Their presence in the Mother Country was giving rise to neo-Nazism, and even the Netherlands, considered a socialistic country, had elected two Nazis from Rotterdam.

"You see where they bomb the Club Med; they going to chase the tourists away. Bad as the economy is. They say they want to chase our foreign friends away, but can they run it? No. This place will end up looking like Haiti, I tell you. I told the president he should crack their coconut heads. They mess up." Some of the young radicals had been rounded up by the police, who were imported from the Mother Country.

"They're nothing but a bunch of illiterate peasants," Martha said. She had been an illiterate peasant herself at one time, hanging her one and only dress on the clothesline each day and trying to make do with a ragged child under a leaking corrugated tin roof. It had all changed after the contest between her and her only rival, Abiahu.

"They want independence. What they know 'bout independence? Who in their right minds would give them a nation? Way it is now, we a part of the Mother Country. The shelves in the stores are full. There's plenty of petrol, perfume, fashions." Johnnie Kranshaw was picking at her soup. Ian could tell that she was embarrassed. He'd seen her name in the newspapers in connection with benefits for left-wing causes. Reading for political prisoners and the millions starving in the Third World. Noticing her discomfort at hearing his mother's views, he changed the subject.

"Ms. Kranshaw," he began. "I know that the thousands of your fans would like to know where you disappeared to. You'd become a mother goddess of the feminist movement. And then, at the height of your success, poof," he said with a wave of his hand. His mother gazed at his hands. Articulate, expressive like his father's. He was huge and muscular like his father, too, and had prodigious lips, and a snug nose. Johnnie Kranshaw leaned back. The Caribbean magic seemed to have brought her peace. The photos on her *Playbills* made her look combative.

"Every time I run into an American at the hotel, they ask me that," she said.

"I'm sorry," Ball said. "I didn't mean to be intrusive—"

"She has a right to keep her business to herself," his mother said, placing her hand gently atop Johnnie Kranshaw's. They looked each other in the eye.

"It's all right, Martha," Johnnie Kranshaw finally said. "I know that many a night I've asked myself that question over at that tourist trap with a view. Chain smoking. If it wasn't for your mother inviting me out here on weekends I don't know what I'd do." The maid entered. She came and picked up the soup bowls and placed them on a tray. Martha was glaring at her. The maid's hands were trembling. Johnnie Kranshaw continued: "They should put a skull and crossbones label on the elixir bottle of success in the United States. It's thrilling, all right. The interviews, being recognized on the street, having credit cards, meeting people you've seen in *People* magazine, the special treatment at the hotels, favors piling up in your mailbox and people asking you to endorse things. Success in the United States is like the potent rum you have down here, makes you want to do the Soca all night. It gives your soul a gorgeous feeling, but the next morning you have a hangover."

The three of them laughed. Like Tremonisha Smarts' plays, her plays were grim, even though the fellas called her a clown. He remembered the cruel things that he and the fellas had said about her. "I should have known when [she mentioned the name of the leading feminist critic] called me 'seductive' and 'ravishing' something must have been up. I should have heeded the warning signs. You know, in the original version of my play *No Good Man*, the man and wife get back together at the end. Becky changed the play so that it had the wife running off with another woman." Ian cleared his throat. He began to have a coughing spasm. "Anything wrong, son?" his mother asked. "No," he said.

"I went along with the program. I didn't care what black men and women were saying about me. Why should I? They hardly attended the theaters where my plays were shown, but they always had plenty of opinions." When she said *black men* she looked at Ian. He looked down at the plate. It was a dish from Guadaloupe, some sort of fish with curry. Ian was beginning to miss the States. He could do with a hamburger along about now. They had a Wendy's and a Burger King in town. They were informal embassies where the youth went to practice their American styles. They wore jeans and played Prince and George Clinton on their radios. McDonald's now occupied a fortress building that had been used by the Mother Country during wars waged by Europeans over the spoils of New Oyo.

He continued to listen to Johnnie Kranshaw's narrative. She had a wholesome figure, he could tell, and for fifty-two years of age she still had all the stuff in the right places. He'd never made it with anybody over fifty, but the fellows say that after making it with a fifty-year-old you don't want none of these young women who have the devil with a red mouth where their pussies should be. He wondered how it would be if he was holding her titties and giving it to her from behind, maintaining his pleasure by concentrating on something dull. He wondered how it would be to give her what the Germans call a *durchficken*. He put it out of his mind. Besides, the only lover she seemed to be fucking was the Caribbean sun.

"One day I was having lunch with Becky at the Four Seasons, and during the course of our conversation I asked her to see if she could get a friend of mine's book published. The book was about natural childbirth and the black community, and do you know what she said?" His mother and Ian stopped eating. They definitely were interested in what Johnnie Kranshaw was going to say.

"Boy, did that bitch get hot. She turned red as a beet, and started talking so loud some of the other people in the restaurant started looking our way. She said that neither she nor her friends in publishing would have anything to do with a book whose subject matter was even remotely connected to the penis.

"She said that the penis had been used as a weapon against all women for thousands of years and that there would be no peace in the world as long as men were not disarmed of their penises." The fellas were right about Becky, Ian thought.

"What did you say?" Martha asked. Johnnie Kranshaw closed her eyes and transmitted her answer to Becky. "I turned to the bitch, cool as you can be, and I said, 'Heifer, you wouldn't even be here if it wasn't for some man's thing.'"

"Well, what did she do?" Martha asked.

"She ran out of the restaurant. Well, two days went by and I was worried about her, I mean she used to call me every day. So I called the office and they told me that she had left instructions that I never call her at home again. Two weeks later, my photo was supposed to appear on the cover of *MaMa*, you know, the big feminist magazine. They had Tremonisha's picture on there and said that just as surely as Eddie Murphy had replaced Richard Pryor, Tremonisha would take my place. They took back all of the praise they'd heaped upon *No Good Man*, and next thing I know, nobody in New York was doing my work. And Becky had said that my play was the most important play of the 1980s, but I just picked up her biography, *Pilgrim's Daughter*, and I'm not even in the index. I read about this package that a travel agency had for Caribbean travel and came down here for two weeks. I stayed. And thanks to your mother and her friends, I've met some people who respect me for what I am." She burst into tears. Martha Ball rose, went over to her and comforted her. Ball was embarrassed. He thought of all the pressure her play *No Good Man* had put on the fellas.

"What's wrong with American women," Martha said. "One of the students from Mother Country University who comes to visit me said that she went to some women's conference in Copenhagen and there were these women from all over the world. They were talking about poverty and birth control and infant mortality. She said that all the American women wanted to talk about was sex. And I read in one of the Miami papers that we get down here that Ann Landers conducted a poll of American women and found that over seventy percent said they didn't like to get fucked, oh, excuse my French," Martha Ball said.

"Penetration," Johnnie Kranshaw said. "They said that they are opposed to penetration. They want to be cuddled. And hugged. Charlene Hatcher Polite was right. They ain't nothin' but a bunch of brat women. They're the most privileged women on earth, but all they do is complain."

"Maybe that's why the American man is always prowling the world with his warships. He can't find no sexual satisfaction at home so he uses these military exercises as a cover for finding exotic women, women that will give him the pleasure he don't get at home. They been leaving those Anglo women since the Crusades, going over into the Arabian countries, raping women. Trying to find women who won't give them none of that 'Dear, I have a headache tonight.' Look at all the different kinds of babies that the Caucasian man has left all over the world. Ian, how do you get along with American women?" his mother asked.

"Oh," Ian said, nervously, "I don't have time to go on

dates. I'm too busy trying to . . . well . . . you know, go for it." His mother frowned.

"He means, he wants to be a success," Johnnie Kranshaw explained.

"He speaks so much of that American language that he's forgotten the Mother Tongue. Wears his hat at the dinner table."

"It's okay, Martha, it's a cowboy hat. Many American men wear them and sometimes won't remove them even when they're going to bed. They sleep and die with their boots on." He removed his hat.

"Thank you," his mother said, squinting her eyes with annoyance. The two women began some small talk. Where there were bargains in downtown New Oyo, where there were some sales going on. They spent time at the beaches and on the tennis courts. That is, when Martha wasn't giving advice to the high and mighty, running events of the country through the president. He wondered were they sleeping together. And Johnnie Kranshaw. She went to lectures and to museums. Had become almost a student of the indigenous dance.

Ball skipped the dessert. Down here they put sugar and rum into everything. It was still a sugar plantation economy. Sure the lavish estates had become tourist restaurants. They were operated by the original plantation owners. They still kept it all in the family, but the president had a black face, and so they didn't fear the uprisings of the former ages, led by men possessed by Orishas.

"Now this is coffee. This is one thing about New Oyo I missed," he said, taking a sip of the coffee from a tiny cup.

"You see, I told you that they've made him into . . . into . . . an American," his mother said, nearly in tears.

"Look, Ma, I didn't mean it that way."

"The *Tribune* said that Tremonisha was the first director of your play. What happened to her?" Johnnie asked.

"She was getting hassled in New York. Seems that she

couldn't please anybody, catching it from all sides, the brothers and the sisters, and then she had a fight with Becky; and Randy Shank—he tied her up and shaved off her hair. Didn't you hear down here? He was going around shaving off the hair of feminists whom, he felt, were smearing the reputations of black men."

"He what?"

"Didn't you hear in the newspapers? He pulled a gun on a cop and was killed after trying to assault Becky French."

"I can't believe it," Johnnie said, her mouth open.

"Sure, he got to twelve women before they caught him."

"His greatest role," Johnnie said.

"Who is this man you're talking about? He sounds crazy to me. Why hadn't they locked him up? If we would have caught him down here we would have given him the African treatment," Martha said.

"He was actually harmless. A brilliant playwright. Some have called him the first modern black playwright," said Johnnie.

"He would dress in a leather coat and matching beret. He wore a mask. Said that he was using a method that the Resistance used after World War Two. Shaving the heads of those who collaborated with the Nazis." Martha started to laugh and wouldn't stop until Johnnie reprimanded her.

"It's not funny, Martha. You don't know how hard it is to be a black person of consciousness in the United States."

"After lecturing his victims, he'd gather up their hair and place it into a black plastic bag," Ball said sadly, shaking his head. He'd begun to admire Randy Shank on the sly.

"Poor Randy," Johnnie said. His mother burst out laughing again; Johnnie glared at her. She stopped.

"Anyway, Tre relocated in Yuba City, California, which according to the *Rand McNally Encyclopedia* is the worst city in the United States. She's begun a theater group out there.

"Old yellow squeaky bitch. They brought her in to take my place because she wouldn't stand up to them. You know how weak those yellow bitches are. They worse than white women."

"You're right about that," Martha said. She was reddish brown.

Good grief, Ball thought. Not only did the black and brown ones hate the white ones, but the yellow ones and each other as well.

"Well, she was asking for it. Writing all of those things, putting down the brothers." Ball looked at her. He started to say what the fellas said. That Johnnie Kranshaw had started the whole thing. The fellas had accused Kranshaw of being the first to dredge up the old black beast image that had horrified and titillated southerners in the 1890s. Johnnie Kranshaw, Tremonisha, and the rest were accused of teasing the public with the old "a fate worse than death." Dangling the gorilla, as the practice is called. Ball changed the subject.

"What are you working on now?"

"Whatever it is, it's hard to drag her away from that hotel, she's so much into it. The woman types day and night," Martha said.

"I never discuss my projects," Johnnie answered. "Let's just say that I'm writing plays from now on that I wouldn't be ashamed to read before a black Baptist Sunday morning worshiping service at Fort Sumter, South Carolina. I'm not going to be used any more by the likes of Becky French." That's it, blame it all on the white woman, Ball thought. "Wasn't enough that we raised their children, cleaned their houses, gave them counsel, and sometimes shared their husbands, now these old crazy white women want us to be pimps for them. After they finished with *No Good Man*, it became nothing but a recruitment poster for lesbianism." Why didn't you stand up to them, Ball thought. Why weren't you as hard on them as you were on the fellas.

"Now that Tre has left, I wonder who Becky's whore is now."

Ball dropped his cup. The coffee left a big spot on the rug.

"Must be jet lag," he said, smiling weakly. His mother called the maid, making awful comments about the maid's color in the Mother Tongue. Ian was glad that Johnnie Kranshaw didn't get a translation. The maid rushed in like a scared rabbit and began to clean up the spilled coffee. His mother finally rose from the table.

"Ian, I'm going upstairs to begin unpacking your clothes. I'll leave you and Johnnie to your playwriting talk."

She left them, lifted her skirts and climbed the stairs toward his bedroom. It had remained the same since he'd left the Island of New Oyo for the States in the mid-seventies. There was a huge photo on the wall of Ball in his rugby shirt and shorts playing soccer. A framed degree in drama from New Oyo University, his books. She'd always scolded him for living in a fantasy world, for being ethereal, but now he had put his fantasies to work. Fantasies can't earn a dime if they only exist in your mind, was her philosophy. That was a nice write-up of *Reckless Eyeballing* in the international edition of the *Herald Tribune*. She laughed. He was just like his father. Crazy. He had his father's Olmec face, his adobe-colored skin, and his gray eyes. One day after the political passions—the violent style of New Oyo's politics—had cooled, she would tell him. She would tell him that she had lied when she said that his father was a shark fisherman who died when his fishing boat capsized. It was one elaborate and entertaining lie. She even said that they'd found his father's undigested parts inside the stomachs of several sharks a few days after his father's death. She looked into his mirror. She turned around and placed her hands on her waist. It was a little thick but in good shape for someone her age. Muscles firm. Superb bone structure, clean jaw line. Her hair streaked with black and red and resembling a large furry hat worn in Siberia. Yakish. Pupils, eight-ball black surrounded by white that resembled the unpolluted clouds above the Atlantic. Large white teeth, the lower lip heavier than the upper one. Huge bosom like Celia Cruz. Yes, indeed, Tina Turner had inspired the women of her age. She walked toward his luggage, which lay at the foot of his bed where the boy had placed it. She opened the first piece. It was his toilet bag and it was full of American products. Aspirin, Ban roll-on, Crest toothpaste, Aqua Velva aftershave. She removed the cap and smelled it. It stank. A toothbrush that had the word *Gum* written on it. Its fibers were soft.

One day, when all of his enemies were dead, she would tell him that Koffee Martin was his father, still a controversial figure since his death in the 1950s. If they knew that he was Martin's son they would kill him too. When she thought of Koffee Martin, Ball's father, her insides would ache. Could he make love. Making love to that man was what making love to chocolate or rum would be like if they could assume a human form. Made you feel sweet and warm inside. Made you tingle all over. But his first wife wouldn't let him go. You know how some of these grudgeful-hearted and malicious colored women refer to the men as their men. Our men. They accuse other women of trying to take "my man." A legacy of the old plantation days when the white planter used the women to control the men. She decided that if she couldn't have him that I couldn't have him. She and Martha were the only people in New Oyo with the Indian gift, the gift of second sight, but because she was blacker and had better public relations she had a bigger following. She always got her police to put Martha in jail for sorcery. She was one of those evil black ones who made a man feel as though he were making love to the night. A Nubian beauty who had a razor's mark that extended from the corner of her left eye down to her chin. She went to the authorities and told them that Koffee was smuggling guns into the country. Koffee had to leave the country in 1940 and go to New York.

Martha Ball removed her son's athletic socks, ten pairs of jeans, and an equal number of jerseys, some of which bore an alligator insignia. He had about eighteen pairs of new jockey shorts.

Koffee gained a great following in the United States, feeding people in his socialistic kitchens at the end of the Depression, turning away no one, black, white, man, woman or child. Thousands of people turned out to see him in Detroit, Cleveland, and Washington, D.C. But he had enemies there as well, enemies who resented his physical features, his accent, enemies who didn't like the fact that this foreigner had such power over their masses. They had him arrested on trumped-up charges and deported him to New Oyo. The Mother Country soldiers took him right from the plane to jail. That night Martha bribed one of the black guards to let her in to see him. The next day he was found dead in his cell. Shortly after she left, they'd come in and beat him until his head resembled a crushed watermelon. When she entered the cell she was one, but when she left Koffee she was one going on two. When Abiahu, his first wife, found out that Martha was pregnant with Ian, she told everybody that she'd put a hex on the child and that he would be born a two-head, of two minds, the one not knowing what the other was up to.

She opened another bag. It was full of audio and video cassettes which included *Shane, High Noon, The Virginian, Bugs Bunny, Donald Duck, Frankenstein, Dracula, The Werewolf of London, Rebel Without a Cause, Superfly.* She opened the garment bag. It held about five winter and spring suits. None looked as if it had ever been worn. There were more cassettes at the bottom of this bag. Larry Holmes vs. Ken Norton, Sugar Ray Robinson vs. Gene Fullmer, Sugar Ray Leonard vs. Thomas Hearns. She stopped for a moment and sat on the bed. Boy just as soon take out American citizenship, she thought. When he was born she and the midwives had taken seriously Abiahu's threat and placed some of that Hebrew obeah around the room. The Hebrews call it *kimpezettl.* They hung it around in case that woman Abiahu tried something funny. They dressed in white and knelt about his bed, praying to the old God, the one before Christ, Muhammad, and Buddha. It must have worked because Ian grew up with no signs of two-headedness or two-facedness. Excelled in Latin. Sent to the school for the elite. Used to have such nice manners before he went to the United States. Spoke the Mother Tongue flawlessly. An aristocrat. The fencing team. Equestrian. And the soccer team. But he wasn't all athlete. Had the green fingers. Could he bring up a flower, and that favorite flower of his, the chrysanthemum, that smelly flower, people said couldn't grow down here, but he grew it. That greenhouse that she built for him out back. He used to go all over the island, giving away chrysanthemums. Chrysanthemums became his calling card. I bet he doesn't remember any of that, and then he went away to America. Started coming home with jazz records and nasty magazines. Naked women in them. Started smoking filthy cigarettes. She sighed. Came home once with some book called *The Tropics Have Cancer.* She couldn't remember the exact title. One nasty book, and then the fast foods and the American cars he had to have. She went over to the last bag, a green army bag, that he sometimes used to carry his belongings. She opened it. It smelled sour. Inside was a dirty, crumpled leather coat. A beret. A dirty white air force scarf, and a black mask. Underneath this she found human hair. Many textures and colors. Fuzzy, frizzy straight, silky, stringy, brittle. "Johnnie, come up here. I need your help," she screamed. Johnnie came into the room from downstairs, quickly. Martha showed her the contents of the bag. "I told you that they have made my child into an American," she said. Downstairs, Ian was staring at a picture in the *Life* magazine's World War II special issue. The picture showed a group of smiling soldiers. They held signs that said "Peace." Upstairs it sounded as though his mother was crying. Ian yelled up:

"Hey, Ma. Is there anything wrong?" Without lifting his head from the magazine. In some photos, people were waving white flags.

LANNAN SELECTIONS

The Lannan Foundation, located in Santa Fe, New Mexico, is a family foundation whose funding is focused on special cultural projects and ideas which promote and protect cultural freedom, diversity, and creativity.

The literary aspect of Lannan's cultural program supports the creation and presentation of exceptional English language literature and develops a wider audience for poetry, fiction, and nonfiction.

Since 1990, the Lannan Foundation has supported Dalkey Archive Press projects in a variety of ways, including monetary support for authors, audience development programs, and direct funding for the publication of the Press's books.

In 2000, Lannan Selections was established to promote both organizations' commitment to the highest expressions of literary creativity. The foundation supports the publication of this series of books each year, and works closely with the Press to ensure that these books will reach as many readers as possible and achieve a permanent place in literature.

DALKEY ARCHIVE PAPERBACKS

PIERRE ALBERT-BIROT, *Grabinoulor.*
YUZ ALESHKOVSKY, *Kangaroo.*
FELIPE ALFAU, *Chromos.*
  Locos.
  Sentimental Songs.
ALAN ANSEN,
  Contact Highs: Selected Poems 1957-1987.
DJUNA BARNES, *Ladies Almanack.*
  Ryder.
JOHN BARTH, *LETTERS.*
  Sabbatical.
AUGUSTO ROA BASTOS, *I the Supreme.*
ANDREI BITOV, *Pushkin House.*
ROGER BOYLAN, *Killoyle.*
CHRISTINE BROOKE-ROSE, *Amalgamemnon.*
GERALD BURNS, *Shorter Poems.*
GABRIELLE BURTON, *Heartbreak Hotel.*
MICHEL BUTOR,
  Portrait of the Artist as a Young Ape.
JULIETA CAMPOS,
  The Fear of Losing Eurydice.
ANNE CARSON, *Eros the Bittersweet.*
LOUIS-FERDINAND CÉLINE, *Castle to Castle.*
  London Bridge.
  North.
  Rigadoon.
HUGO CHARTERIS, *The Tide Is Right.*
JEROME CHARYN, *The Tar Baby.*
MARC CHOLODENKO, *Mordechai Schamz.*
EMILY HOLMES COLEMAN,
  The Shutter of Snow.
ROBERT COOVER, *A Night at the Movies.*
STANLEY CRAWFORD,
  Some Instructions to My Wife.
RENÉ CREVEL, *Putting My Foot in It.*
RALPH CUSACK, *Cadenza.*
SUSAN DAITCH, *Storytown.*
PETER DIMOCK,
  A Short Rhetoric for Leaving the Family.
COLEMAN DOWELL, *The Houses of Children.*
  Island People.
  Too Much Flesh and Jabez.
RIKKI DUCORNET, *The Complete Butcher's Tales.*
  The Fountains of Neptune.
  The Jade Cabinet.
  Phosphor in Dreamland.
  The Stain.
WILLIAM EASTLAKE, *Castle Keep.*
  Lyric of the Circle Heart.
STANLEY ELKIN, *Boswell: A Modern Comedy.*
  Criers and Kibitzers, Kibitzers and Criers.

  The Dick Gibson Show.
  The MacGuffin.
  The Magic Kingdom.
ANNIE ERNAUX, *Cleaned Out.*
LAUREN FAIRBANKS, *Muzzle Thyself.*
  Sister Carrie.
LESLIE A. FIEDLER,
  Love and Death in the American Novel.
RONALD FIRBANK, *Complete Short Stories.*
FORD MADOX FORD, *The March of Literature.*
JANICE GALLOWAY, *Foreign Parts.*
  The Trick Is to Keep Breathing.
WILLIAM H. GASS, *The Tunnel.*
  Willie Masters' Lonesome Wife.
ETIENNE GILSON, *The Arts of the Beautiful.*
C. S. GISCOMBE, *Giscome Road.*
  Here.
KAREN ELIZABETH GORDON, *The Red Shoes.*
PATRICK GRAINVILLE, *The Cave of Heaven.*
GEOFFREY GREEN, ET AL., *The Vineland Papers.*
HENRY GREEN, *Concluding.*
  Nothing.
JIŘÍ GRUŠA, *The Questionnaire.*
JOHN HAWKES, *Whistlejacket.*
ALDOUS HUXLEY, *Antic Hay.*
  Point Counter Point.
  Those Barren Leaves.
  Time Must Have a Stop.
GERT JONKE, *Geometric Regional Novel.*
TADEUSZ KONWICKI, *A Minor Apocalypse.*
  The Polish Complex.
ELAINE KRAF, *The Princess of 72nd Street.*
EWA KURYLUK, *Century 21.*
DEBORAH LEVY, *Billy and Girl.*
JOSÉ LEZAMA LIMA, *Paradiso.*
OSMAN LINS, *The Queen of the Prisons of Greece.*
ALF MAC LOCHLAINN,
  The Corpus in the Library.
  Out of Focus.
D. KEITH MANO, *Take Five.*
BEN MARCUS, *The Age of Wire and String.*
WALLACE MARKFIELD, *Teitlebaum's Window.*
  To an Early Grave.
DAVID MARKSON, *Collected Poems.*
  Reader's Block.
  Springer's Progress.
  Wittgenstein's Mistress.
CARL R. MARTIN, *Genii Over Salzburg.*
CAROLE MASO, *AVA.*
HARRY MATHEWS, *Cigarettes.*
  The Conversions.

Visit our website: www.dalkeyarchive.com

DALKEY ARCHIVE PAPERBACKS

Visit our website: www.dalkeyarchive.com